BY RICHARD J. LOWE

Shieldmaiden Tales

Fire in the North

Clans of the Silver Hills

Beyond the Sunset Isles

Feybane

Science Fiction

Box

RICHARD J. LOWE

Feybane

Copyright © Richard J Lowe 2020
All rights reserved

First published in paperback by Richard J Lowe in 2020

http://www.facebook.com/richardjloweauthor/

Cover illustration by Sarah Mercer
http://Sarah-mercer.co.uk/

*With thanks to my advance readers:
Rob, Des, Amanda, and my mother, Susan.*

CHAPTER 1

Maena raised the sacrificial dagger high above her head and uttered the final words of summoning. She paused, her arms trembling ever so slightly, then drove the blade downwards.

Her victim's end was soundless apart from the thump of the knife impacting meat. Maena wanted no noisy screaming disrupting the ceremony, so she had given the young female dwarf a powerful sleeping draught before the servants carried the sacrifice to the stone altar. She had considered using a goat, but the demands of the blood magic being used in this ritual were too high for an animal to suffice.

She was now standing next to the altar in the middle of the ancient stone circle. Maena had dismissed the servants before beginning the ritual. It was only right that she alone witnessed her King's return.

Blood welled from the dying dwarf's chest and pooled on the rough surface of the stone altar. There was a crack of thunder and a jagged fork of lightning leapt from dark grey clouds to strike a nearby tree. The tree burst into flames throwing a second set of shadows from the standing stones across the altar. A low rumble followed the thunder, but this time it was coming from under her feet. The ground shook, and Maena released the dagger, leaving it protruding from the sacrifice's chest. She grabbed at the altar to steady herself but her hand slipped off, coming away slick with the sacrifice's blood.

The clouds over the stone circle glowed a deep green as the tremors intensified, and she staggered over to one of the stones that made up the circle and leant against it for support.

The ground cracked and fissures radiated out from the stone altar. Maena took a step back as steam started to billow out of the ragged tears in the ground. Despite her earlier confidence while performing the ritual she was beginning to feel a little unsure of this whole situation and followed stepping back with ducking behind the relative safety of the standing stone.

The rumbling reached a crescendo, the ground heaved violently, and Maena lost her balance. With a little cry, she fell to her knees.

There was a loud bang and the shaking abruptly stopped. A mixture of soil and rocks was launched into the air from the other side of the standing stone, and Maena threw her hands over her head to protect herself from the cascading rain of debris as it crashed down all around her.

An unnatural quiet descended on the stone circle. Once she was convinced the shaking was not going to restart, she got to her feet and brushed grass from her long, flowing blue dress. Then, she cautiously peered around the side of the stone and couldn't help letting out an involuntary gasp.

The altar was gone, shattered into a million fragments. Standing in the centre of the devastated turf was an imposing figure. At six foot and five inches, he would have been tall for a human, let alone a dwarf. However, he was clearly neither. His almond-shaped eyes were a vivid violet colour and a pair of pointed pink ears were just visible through his long blonde hair. His long green cloak swirled dramatically, giving her flashing glimpses of his smooth, well-muscled legs. He really was quite beautiful thought Maena. She took a deep breath to calm the butterflies that had started in her stomach and stepped out into the open.

'My King.' She dropped into a deep curtsy.

King Oberon turned and regarded her coolly.

Maena straightened out of her curtsy to her full height of four feet. 'Your Queen has returned you to this realm.'

'My Queen?' A shadow of a frown passed across his face. He stared at her intently and Maena felt as if those bright violet eyes were boring into her soul.

'How delicious. A svalfae.' The corner of his mouth turned up in a half-smile.

This wasn't quite the reaction she had hoped for. 'Yes. I am a svalfae, my King.'

'And you expect to be my Queen?'

The direction in which this exchange was heading troubled Maena. 'Yes, my King.'

His laughter was both beautiful and cruel at the same time. 'I remember you, my dear. It is little Maena, isn't it?'

'Yes.'

'And where are the others, Maena? Sweet Andraste and Coventina?' Oberon asked softly.

'I...' Maena hesitated. She locked gaze with Oberon and felt her will slip away. 'They were given the final death, my King.'

'Enterprising. Doing so gives you the right to be my Queen. Is that it?'

'Yes, my King.'

'Ah, you three were always prone to flights of fancy.' Oberon chuckled quietly.

'But whoever returns you to this realm becomes your Queen. We were promised,' said Maena.

'That lie was such a motivator, wasn't it?'

Maena blinked. 'A lie?'

He laughed. 'I'm Oberon, king of the fae. What did you expect? Fairness, truth and justice?'

Maena felt sick to the pit of her stomach. Andraste and Coventina had been right to not want to return Oberon to the world. How could she have been so foolish?

Oberon stepped forward, took one of Maena's blood-soaked hands in his, and gently cupped her chin with his other hand. 'You were always my favourite, Maena. So loyal.'

'Yes, I am loyal to you, my King.'

'Just so. You don't mind if I make sure, do you?'

'Make sure?' she said falteringly.

Oberon dropped her hand and stroked her cheek, leaving a long smear of blood on her face. She remained still as he leaned in close and blew sweet warm breath and a handful of arcane words into her ear.

Maena felt her whole body tingle as if she was being stroked by a hundred different feathers, and her eyelids drooped sensuously as she was washed by pleasure. 'Uh,' was all she managed to say.

Oberon tilted her head up and languidly kissed her. His lips were cool on hers.

'Now then little Maena. Show me to my castle.'

Her head still buzzing from the power of his charm, all Maena could do was nod and lead him down the hill and back to the house.

Maena was sitting at her dressing table by the window looking out over the grounds of her house. She sighed and mentally corrected herself: King Oberon's house. She was effectively a prisoner here; the enchantment used on her by Oberon kept her current vessel within a mile of the ritual circle at the top of the hill.

Maena had come to the realisation that the other svalfae had been right to not return Oberon to this world. Oh, she had been correct to assume he would gather power to bring his rule to the world, but she had been wrong about becoming his Queen to rule by his side. Instead, she was held here by an enchantment and expected to pander to Oberon's every whim. She supposed she should be grateful that the King did not seem to have fully recovered his baser appetites since his return. He had taken her to his bed once and had then mostly ignored her. Maena felt a peculiar mixture of slighted and relieved. She supposed that was caused by the enchantment. It really was bothersome not knowing exactly which emotions and urges were her own. She could sympathise with all those she had used blood magic enchantments on in the past. That sympathy was annoying too. There was some vestige of the shieldmaiden she had shared a body with, Bienia, knocking around in her subconscious.

'Shit.' Maena recognised the irony of using one of the shieldmaiden's favourite swear words to describe what she thought of the situation.

'Mistress?'

Maena turned to see her one remaining aspirant at the open door of the bedroom.

'Nothing, Neave. Just a general observation.' Maena waved one hand around to indicate everything.

'Can I help at all?' asked Neave.

'Why are you still here, Neave?' asked Maena.

She was genuinely curious. When Oberon had broken the blood magic enchantment binding them to Maena, the rest of the aspirants had returned to their families in Basalt and the villages of Saltrock. Oberon's odious redcaps soon replaced them. One of the first things that the King did after he arrived was to create a gateway to the otherworld at the ritual circle. Many years ago, the men of the old Aravic empire banished Oberon and most of his minions to the otherworld, a place similar to the beyond but with more trees and fewer tentacles. Maena had opened a temporary link to the otherworld to bring back Oberon, but this new gateway was permanent, allowing the King to bring hordes of the redcaps through. Shorter, stockier and uglier in both body and spirit than dwarves, they were the most numerous of his servants.

'I decided to stay with you, mistress,' said Neave.

'But you could leave any time you like. Oberon hasn't bothered binding you to him,' said Maena.

'Where else would I go? My place is with you.'

Maena raised an eyebrow. 'I really don't understand you, my dear.'

'Mistress?' Several emotions competed for access to Naeve's face.

'Nevermind. Did you want something?'

Neave said nothing for a moment as 'troubled' won the competition. 'King Oberon requests your presence in his bedchamber,' said Neave.

'And he sent you to tell me.' Maena sighed. 'You know, the King can be a real bastard.'

CHAPTER 2

'You know, the King can be a real bastard,' said Bienia.

'The sodding Astish haven't heard of holiday pay,' said Brynhild.

'He just laughed when I told him it's a long-standing tradition of the dwarven clan armies.'

The two dwarven shieldmaidens were in their natural habitat: the ale room of an inn. It was typical of those found in farming hamlets in the north of Asterland. The furnishings consisted of a few tables, plenty of sawdust on the floor and a couple of kegs behind the bar. The atmosphere could best be described as convivial and smoggy. Loud ale fuelled conversations and swirling banks of aromatic pipe smoke filled the room.

At first glance, the third chair at their table appeared to be empty. However, it was occupied by Pockle the fairy. Barely a foot tall, he could only reach the tabletop by standing on the chair, although he had given up attempting to stand about an hour ago after his fourth bottle of beer. This may not sound like much, but each bottle was almost as tall as him.

'Screw the King.' Pockle hiccuped. 'You two broads are the greatest.' He grabbed the edge of the table with both hands and, with the help of a few flaps of his multi-hued wings, heaved himself to his feet. 'Time for another drink.'

'Another?' asked Brynhild. 'Are you sure?'

'Of corsh I'm sure,' slurred Pockle. Then he fell backwards, landing on his backside with a thump. He lay on his side, using his hands as a pillow and mumbled, 'Just gonna shit here for a bit.'

'What did he just say?' asked Bienia.

Brynhild performed a peculiar mix of a chuckle combined with a belch. 'Oops. 'scuse me.'

'I would declare this evening to be perfect if I could find someone to play Beggar's Five with,' said Bienia.

'Don't look at me. Too much ale in here.' Brynhild patted her stomach. 'You'd take me to the cleaners.'

Bienia sniffed. 'From the smell of you, that wouldn't be a bad idea.'

'Hey!' Brynhild frowned, raised her right arm and gave her armpit an experimental sniff. 'You're right. I stink.' She lowered her arm. 'To be fair, we have been on the road for a week.'

'Not long now, and we'll reach Snorri's.'

Brynhild smiled. 'I wonder how the old goat is doing?'

'Do you think he'll be glad to see Pockle?' asked Bienia.

Brynhild's smile faded. 'I guess Pockle will leave once he knows his debt to Snorri is paid.'

Bienia peered over the edge of the table at the fairy. He was gently snoring. 'Maybe. He seems to be very attached to you.'

'He's a good friend,' said Brynhild.

'I suppose so. He's never weed in your shoes,' said Bienia.

'Hey, it was dark. You shouldn't have left your boots by the door,' said Brynhild.

'No need to get all defensive,' said Bienia.

'Sorry.' Brynhild sighed. 'I'm going to miss him.'

'I know. I'll probably miss the little bastard too.'

'Miss who? He sounds like an arsehole.' Pockle had somehow made it onto the tabletop and was swaying unsteadily from side to side. It looked as if the only thing keeping him upright was an occasional flap of his wings.

Bienia hid her laugh behind her hand.

'You alright, Pockle?' asked Brynhild.

'Fecking right. Yes. I am.' He sat down in a puddle of beer. 'Sploosh,' he said absently.

'That's enough for one night; we have an early start. Come on, time for bed,' said Bienia.

Pockle peered up at Bienia. 'Now there's a fecking offer I can't refuse.' His lecherous smile revealed his needle-sharp teeth.

Bienia rolled her eyes. 'Gods, you're predictable.'

Pockle hiccuped. 'More ale!'

Brynhild adopted a stern expression. 'Bienia is right, Pockle. Time to get some sleep.'

Pockle mournfully looked up at Brynhild. 'Just one more?'

Bienia was glad she wasn't on the end of the stare that Brynhild gave in response.

'Alright, alright. I get the fecking message.' Pockle got to his feet and experimentally flapped his wings. He was swaying from side to side.

'Best if I carry you.' Brynhild tapped her left shoulder.

Pockle held up his arms towards Brynhild as if in supplication to some sort of deity. She obligingly scooped him up and placed him on her shoulder.

Bienia sighed with relief. It could be a chore getting Pockle out of a drinking establishment. They had got off lightly this time.

The shieldmaidens left their table and went to the bar

where the barman was wiping a mug with a dirty cloth. Bienia slapped a handful of coins onto the bar.

The barman picked up the coins and made a show of counting them.

'We'll be wanting breakfast in the morning,' said Bienia.

'All three of you?' The barman was looking at Pockle who was standing on Brynhild's shoulder with his arms outstretched. It sounded like he was singing a song about a little pixie.

'Yes. All three of us.'

'It's just, uh.' The barman hesitated.

'Yes?'

The barman leant forward and whispered, 'What do they eat?'

'He eats raw meat,' said Bienia.

'Raw?'

'Yes, the fresher the better.'

Pockle grinned at the barman. 'A fecking lovely shirloin steak, if you got it.'

The barman flinched at the sight of Pockle's razor sharp smile.

Bienia carefully place a gleaming silver coin on the bar. 'For your trouble.'

The barman swept the coin off the bar and into his pocket. 'Right you are. Two traveller's breakfasts and one raw steak.'

Bienia nodded acknowledgement before the shieldmaidens made their way rather unsteadily to their rooms.

CHAPTER 3

Centuries ago, Lord Avon of Aston, as well as being an alliteratively named ruler, had carved out a kingdom for himself by conquering the lands surrounding Aston, forming a feudal kingdom which he had imaginatively called Asterland. However, he had failed to bring the north under his rule and it was his grandson, King John, who had finally subjugated the north. Now, his great-great-grandson King Stephen was embroiled in the final stages of a civil war with the northern lords. Only Lord Ponder remained, defiantly holding out in Helgal castle which had been under siege for a month.

It was around midnight that the rider from the south arrived and was ushered into the King's command tent. The King and his nobles were planning the assault on Helgal. Someone had gone to the trouble of making a model of the castle and placing tiny carved wooden soldiers along the walls.

The planning session was suspended once the messenger's tidings were revealed.

The news brought a scowl to King Stephen's face. 'Fort May you say?'

'Yes, sire. The nomads had siege engines.'

'Siege engines?' King Stephen's scowl deepened. 'Rychard,

get a full report. I still need to plan tomorrow's assault on Helgal.'

'Yes, your majesty.' Lord Rychard bowed and left the tent with the messenger.

Twenty minutes later, Lord Rychard was in his tent with Luke, his spymaster. They were sitting at a table and drinking red wine from two pewter goblets. A clay jug half filled with wine was in the middle of the table.

'This is consistent with the reports of the warlord Karvarl mustering a large force of nomads and mercenaries near Olong,' said Luke.

'Now we know what he intends to do with it,' said Rychard. 'Couldn't bloody march south could he?'

'I'm afraid the civil war has made Asterland a tempting target,' said Luke.

'So, they will come north.'

'It would seem so,' said Luke.

Lord Rychard drained his goblet and placed it back on the table. 'What agents have we got in his army?'

'Ah,' said Luke.

'Ah? I don't like the sound of that.'

Luke picked up the jug of wine and refilled Lord Rychard's goblet.

'Come on man. What is it?' asked Lord Rychard.

Luke placed the jug back on the table and sighed. 'My lord. As you know, Macky and his team have been our eyes and ears in Olong for many years now.'

'And?'

'I'm afraid we haven't heard from Macky in some time.

His usual contact via the trade road has reported that the dead drop has been empty on his last three visits.'

'Probably a dead man's drop now, eh?'

Luke nodded his head slightly in acknowledgment. 'My lord, you are, as ever, incisive in your observations.'

'Who have we got available? Someone we can trust, I mean.'

'That caveat narrows the field somewhat. But, Julienne and her farm-boy are currently unassigned.'

'Not for long.' Rychard smiled grimly. 'See to it.'

* * *

The city of Aston sprawled in an unruly collection of stone and timber structures along the banks of the river Neet and the Conway estuary. The original walls that surrounded the old city had long ago been swallowed by uncontrolled building and the city was by any military measure, indefensible.

The afternoon sun warmed the terrace of Ganty's Pie and Ale shop, an establishment situated next to the river. The smell drifting up from the water was faint, the odour of the Neet was almost undetectable this far upriver. The Neet was used for most of the cities waste, so the further downriver a house was, the poorer its inhabitants and conversely the further upriver the wealthier. King Stephen's father had started a project to dig sewers like those found in Port Denly, but they were never completed. The resulting haphazard sewer coverage of the city was due to a combination of the money running out and disruptive action by the local gong farmers. These pillars of the community had organised themselves to oppose something that was taking away their livelihood and had successfully prosecuted a campaign of petty sabotage that hindered the development of the planned sanitation works. It was upriver that had the more complete sewer network.

Julienne leant over and used a napkin to wipe an errant piece of pie crust from John's mouth. 'It won't last, you know.'

'Why not?'

'Two reasons. One: our hazard pay will run out if we keep eating like this, and two: him.' Julienne pointed over John's shoulder.

John turned his head to see a well-dressed, slender man approaching their table.

'Who's he?'

Julienne sighed, then deployed one of her winning smiles. 'Hello, Alphonse.'

'Alphonse? What sort of a name is that?' muttered John. Fortunately, the man didn't hear him or was choosing to ignore John's observation.

'Barbara, how delightful to see you,' said Alphonse.

He was clearly talking to Julienne. Barbara was obviously another of Julienne's pseudonyms. John couldn't place the man's accent. Maybe it was from the lands that lay to the south of the Pockveld.

'Alfy, dahling,' said Julienne.

John could place that accent. Pure upriver Aston.

'Do come and join us,' said Julienne.

'I'm afraid I can't stay for long.' Alphonse pulled a chair over from a nearby table and sat down.

Julienne held her hand out to Alphonse. 'Do tell me you can at least stay for dessert?'

John decided that keeping quiet was his best move. He suspected Alphonse was not as he appeared. Julienne certainly wasn't.

Alphonse took the proffered hand in both his and shook his head. 'I am afraid not my lady, though it grieves me to say so.'

Julienne pulled her hand back. 'You shouldn't disappoint me like that.'

'I am sorry, Barbara. You know how it is.' Alphonse smiled wryly. 'No rest for the wicked.'

'Well, it is a pity.'

'It is.' Alphonse stood and turned as if noticing John for the first time. 'A pleasure to meet you, Barbara's dinner date.'

'Uh. Yeah. Likewise,' said John.

Julienne patted Alphonse's arm. 'Don't be a stranger, dear.'

'I apologise that I could not stay. Farewell.' Alphonse bowed deeply and then left the terrace.

'Well, he was odd,' said John.

'He was one of Luke's men,' said Julienne.

She had a small scrap of paper in the palm of her hand which she was eyeing suspiciously.

'What is it?' asked John.

'Play time's over. We're going to Olong.'

'Olong? Where the hell is that?' asked John.

'That way,' said Julienne pointing vaguely south. She looked at John appraisingly then looked back at the note. 'First, we need to go shopping.'

* * *

After a busy afternoon haggling over the price of some arms and armour, they returned to their inn room. Instead of going to a reputable armourer and having fitted armour made in his size, Julienne had insisted they trawl the pawn shops on Pec Street looking for equipment that had been scavenged from the battlefield. Now John was trying all the disparate pieces of armour together for the first time, and he could feel every misfitting strap, buckle and armour plate.

Julienne was assisting him with the breastplate.

'Not too tight,' said John.

'Stop being a baby.'

There was one more tug and Julienne slapped the breastplate. 'And you're done. How does it feel?'

'Really uncomfortable. I don't know how Bienia wears this sort of stuff all the time.'

He realised comfort would be a thing of the past once they embarked on their new mission. Army camps were not known for luxurious accommodation. He looked sadly at the inn-room's invitingly comfy bed. He would miss it.

Julienne followed his gaze and grinned wickedly. 'No time for that. Besides, I didn't spend all this time putting your armour on you to just take it all back off again.'

John flexed his hands. They felt clumsy in the steel-plated gauntlets. 'What's my cover again?'

'You're a mercenary looking to join up with the warlord Karvarl's army. You've been fighting in the Astish civil war for one of the northern lords and are looking for new work.'

'Which northern lord?'

'Your choice. Just not Lord Ponder because he hasn't surrendered yet.'

'Umm, how about Trent?'

Julienne nodded. 'Good choice. A dead minor noble. Less likely to run into anyone else who fought for him.'

'You haven't told me what your cover story is yet.'

'Now don't go getting any ideas, but I'm going to be your servant,' said Julienne.

John smiled broadly. 'My serving wench?'

'Servant,' said Julienne.

'Serving wench sounds better.'

Julienne brushed his cheek with her hand. 'Don't push it, lover.'

'Alright. Servant it is. What names are we using?'

'We stick to John and Julienne. Nobody knows us down there, and you're less likely to screw up and use the wrong name.'

'Your faith in me is awe-inspiring,' said John.

Julienne headed off his impending grumpiness with a swift kiss on the cheek. 'I just know you, my sweet.'

John picked up a battered pot-helmet from the sideboard and turned it over in his hands. 'This stuff has seen better days.' In a way, he was glad they hadn't asked about what had happened to the previous owner.

'Needs to look used. You're supposed to be an experienced mercenary down on his luck, not a farm-boy in his first suit of armour.'

'Fine.' He put the helmet on and started doing up the chin strip. 'Why am I wearing it now? Can I not just wear it when we get wherever we're going.'

Julienne patted the top of his helmet. 'You need to get used to wearing it. At the moment you're moving like somebody who has had an embarrassing accident in his codpiece.'

'Very funny.'

'I know you love me for my sense of humour. Come on, let's go find some dinner. You can work on that walk on the way.'

CHAPTER 4

Maena did not know what was worse: being peremptorily summoned to Oberon's bedchamber every day, or being ignored for weeks on end as if she didn't exist. It had been almost two months since King Oberon had so much as acknowledged her existence and she was getting bored. There was only so much reading in the house library or sitting about in the garden she could take. Oberon had been planning his glorious invasion of the Sunset Isles and the mainland without her. It was all so intolerable. She had to get out of here.

She looked at her companion dozing in the sun, an empty ale bottle beside her on the garden bench. 'Neave.'

There was no response. Maena shoved the young dwarf's arm. 'Neave,' she repeated.

'Huh? What?' Neave rubbed her eyes then realised where she was and bowed her head in contrition. 'Sorry, mistress.'

Maena waved her hand. 'Yes, yes. You're very sorry for falling asleep. Let's just take your abject apology as read.'

'Mistress?' Neave frowned slightly.

'I have a question about your brother.'

'My brother?'

'Yes. The slow one. Smells of goats. Had a thing for that shieldmaiden,' said Maena.

'Hevac?'

'That's the one. Does he still visit you?'

'Sometimes. He tries to convince me to go back to the farm with him.'

'Of course he does,' said Maena. 'Bring him to me the next time he visits.'

Neave bowed her head in acquiescence. 'Yes, mistress.'

Maena was sitting at her window looking out at the gardener giving the animal topiary a trim. The gardener was one of the few servants that hadn't been replaced by a redcap. The diminutive terrorists did not have any horticultural aptitude, and the topiary fox in the south-east corner of the grounds was only barely recognisable as a creature of the forest after their attempt to emulate the gardener's efforts.

She sniffed at the robust aroma of goat that had invaded her bedchamber. Then stopped, coughing. When she turned away from the window, she was not surprised to find Hevac nervously shuffling from one foot to the other in the middle of her bedchamber. Neave stood behind him trying not to look mortally embarrassed.

'Ah, the goatherd,' said Maena.

'You asked that I bring my brother to see you, mistress,' said Neave.

'I did. Tell me Neave, would you do anything for me?'

'Yes, of course.' The devotion in Naeve's eyes was obvious.

'And Hevac. Would you do anything for your sister?'

The burly goatherd glanced at Neave before answering. 'Yes.'

Maena hoped she hadn't misjudged the goatherd. 'I need you to help me.'

Hevac said nothing. Neave stepped towards him and placed a hand on his shoulder. 'Please, Hevac.'

'Helping me will enable Neave to return to the farm,' said Maena.

Neave dropped her hand from Hevac's shoulder. 'Mistress?'

Maena arched her left eyebrow. 'You will do this for me?'

There was barely any hesitation from Neave. 'Yes, mistress.'

'And you, goatherd. Will you assist me and enable your sister to return to your farm?'

There was considerably more hesitation from Hevac. 'Yes,' he said deliberately.

'Good.' Maena walked to her dresser, opened a drawer, and pulled out her favourite sacrificial dagger.

Hevac flinched away from the weapon as Maena approached the siblings.

'Neave.' Maena beckoned impatiently.

Neave held out her arm with no hesitation and rolled back her sleeve. The back of her forearm was criss-crossed with pale white scars.

'Neave, what's going on?' asked Hevac.

'I am assisting my mistress with her magic.'

Maena carefully drew the dagger across the skin of the dwarf's arm. Blood welled out of the cut and she wiped the flat of the blade across the wound smearing it with blood.

Hevac started to take a step back, but Neave held him in place with her free hand. 'Don't move, brother.'

Maena recited the ancient words of blood-magic that

would transfer her consciousness to another vessel. Hevac wasn't prepared, so she couldn't wipe him clean, but at least she could ensure she was the dominant personality. Not like the transfer she had performed on the shieldmaiden, Bienia, as her vessel had died. That had been a decidedly frustrating year being relegated to observer in another's body.

She felt the familiar shock of transferral lace her body. Half agony, half ecstasy.

The last thing she saw through this vessel's eyes were Hevac's dark brown eyes regarding her fearfully.

Then she was looking at her vessel crumpling to the floor. The dagger clattered from the vessel's limp fingers as Maena instinctively reached out and gathered her into her arms. Her arms. Which were muscular and not a little hairy. This was going to take some getting used to.

She heard Hevac's voice just above her ears, somewhere in the back of her head. '*Hey, what's going on?*'

She aimed her thoughts inside. Don't worry. This is only temporary.

'*Temporary? I don't understand what's going on. Why can't I move my arms?*'

She ignored him for now. He would either work it out or he wouldn't. It didn't really matter. The important thing was to put her plan into effect.

'Neave. We must leave for Basalt.' Maena caught herself before she tried to clear her throat. Hevac's annoyingly calm and simple voice was lower than she was used to.

'Hevac, put her on the bed please,' said Neave.

Maena realised she was still holding on to her previous vessel. 'Yes. Help me put her into bed.'

With Neave's help they soon had the empty vessel tucked into bed.

'Come. Now we must go.' She scooped her dagger from the floor, jamming it into the wide leather belt worn by the goatherd.

'But I cannot leave,' said Neave.

Maena wished she had thought to explain her plan to Neave before enacting it.

'Your plan? Enacting? Am I a prisoner in my own body?'

'Yes. You can leave, Neave. I am your mistress.'

Neave did not immediately respond. Her mouth opened and closed a couple of times as if she was having trouble forming any words. Thankfully, Hevac was also now being silent.

Maena tried to smile comfortingly. 'I have taken your brother as a temporary vessel.'

'Hevac, mistress? I didn't know...' Neave tailed off, a mixture of shock and confusion written across her face.

'That I could transfer to a male? It's not my first choice of destination, but needs must.'

'But Hevac...'

'Your brother is fine,' said Maena. This voice would take some getting used to.

'Fine? I'm not sure I'd describe myself as fine.'

'Well, as fine as can be expected, under the circumstances,' Maena amended.

'If you say so, mistress.' Neave still wore a troubled frown.

'And Neave,' said Maena.

'Yes, mistress?'

'You're going to need to stop calling me mistress.'

'Yes, mi—' Neave stopped. 'Then what should I call you?'

Maena spread her thick, hairy arms wide. 'May as well call me Hevac.'

'Yes... Hevac. This is very strange.'

'*You're telling me,*' said Hevac.

'You'll get used to it. Now we should get out of here before Oberon gets a good look at the goatherd.' Maena looked down at her new vessel. 'I mean me.'

CHAPTER 5

The trip to Basalt had gone smoothly. Pretending to be a simple goatherd had been harder than she had expected, but nobody seemed to notice her occasional slip into 'imperious svalfae'. Neave was quite adept at diverting any suspicion, explaining that her brother was a bit strange in the head and they were going to see a doctor in Basalt. Now they had to get on a ship and away from Saltrock.

Maena and Neave were sitting at a table outside the Salty Dog tavern looking out across the water. There were more ships than usual in the harbour. King Oberon had ordered all returning merchant ships to remain. He had not given his reasons, but Maena suspected they were to be used as transports for the hordes of redcaps that had been coming through the gate to the otherworld.

'I can tell a Captain to take us,' said Neave.

'Perhaps.' Maena knew this idea was not without merit. After all, Neave was an aspirant. Even after King Oberon had corrupted the town stones, there was enough residual blood magic enchantment on the dwarves of Saltrock for them to obey an aspirant unquestioningly. They had found this out in the pub when Neave did not have to pay for their meal and lodging.

'There is one now. I will go and tell him.' Neave stood up.

'Sit down. I think a more subtle approach is required,' said Maena.

'Subtle, mistress?'

'Yes. We shall be taken on as crew. This will draw less notice than an aspirant and her idiot brother travelling as honoured passengers. And stop calling me mistress.'

'I understand,' said Neave.

'Go. Talk to the captain,' said Maena.

The dwarf in question was sitting alone at another table nursing a mug of ale. His status as captain was confirmed by his tricorn hat which was pushed back, revealing a weather-beaten face that had seen years at sea. Maena watched his expression carefully as Neave talked to him and breathed a sigh of relief when she saw him nod and shake Neave's hand.

The young dwarf returned to their table and sat down before talking in a low voice. 'The captain was curious as to why an aspirant wanted to sign on as a common sailor.'

'And?' asked Maena.

'I told him not to be. That seemed to work. We are now crew on board the Regal Dolphin.'

'Good,' said Maena. 'You have done well.'

Neave beamed happily. 'Thankyou, mi—Hevac.'

Maena patted her on the arm. 'That's better. We will tell him to leave once we are safely on board.'

'He did mention one thing that may be important,' said Neave.

'And that is?'

'King Oberon ordered all the ship stones to be handed in and stored.'

'Shit,' said Maena. The expletive sounded better in Hevac's deep tones than it ever did in her previous vessel.

'You can enchant another?'

'Yes, but it needs a day long ritual.'

'Oh,' said Neave. 'Sorry.'

'Not your fault, dear. We can perform the ritual on the boat.'

Later that day, the pair boarded the ship. Neave was carrying a small wooden cage which contained a scrawny looking chicken. Its head bobbed as it watched the world go by and it gave an occasional cluck as if in commentary.

Anlon, the ship's first mate, pointed at the poultry. 'And what is that?'

Neave looked at him as if he was stupid. 'It's a chicken.'

'I can see it's a bloody chicken. What are you doing bringing it on board the ship?'

'That is none of your concern,' said Maena.

The first mate shifted his attention to the other newcomer. 'Everything that goes on board is my concern, goat boy. Now, why don't you shut your mouth and get below.'

Having put the goatherd in his place, the first mate shifted his attention back to Neave. 'And as for you—'

There was a cough from behind the angry dwarf and he turned, ready to deliver a barrage of abuse. This was cut short when he saw who was doing the coughing. 'Captain Gallcob,' he said.

The captain beckoned his first mate over and then whispered something in his ear. The perplexed expression on the man's face became tinged with fear as he glanced back at Neave.

Maena, who had been about to put the first mate in his place, refrained from saying anything. She watched quietly as he came back and briefly bowed his head towards Neave before speaking. 'Aspirant. Of course you may keep your chicken on board.'

'Thankyou,' said Neave.

'You can keep it in the aft hold,' said Captain Gallcob.

'Oh, I won't be keeping it,' said Neave.

Captain Gallcob scratched his head. 'Eh?'

'It's for the ritual,' said Neave.

Maena hurriedly interjected. 'Perhaps we should discuss this in private.'

The captain nodded in agreement. 'Yes. We should talk in my cabin. Your man-servant can take the bird to the hold.'

Maena realised she was the man-servant. She could hear an almost imperceptible chuckle in her head. '*That put you in your place.*'

'Fine. Give me the bird.' Maena held out her hand.

Neave hesitantly handed the cage over.

'Aspirant?' Captain Gallcob was stuck in a half bow, his extended arm showing the way to his cabin.

'Yes. Yes, of course. See to it, ah, Hevac,' said Neave.

'Yes, mistress,' said Maena. She couldn't help smirking a little as she used the familiar honorific to address Neave. Fortunately, the captain did not seem to notice.

Neave, slightly flustered, nodded to the captain and went with him to his cabin.

Maena wondered if Neave would take him to her bed.

'*That's my sister! She wouldn't.*'

Maybe Hevac was right. Neave wouldn't consider a dalliance with a member of the lower orders. On the other hand, a captain may be of sufficient rank to qualify as far as social standing went.

'Neave would not do that sort of thing outside of wedlock.'

'Didn't stop you with the shieldmaiden, did it Hevac?' said Maena as she swung the wooden cage down through the hatch.

CHAPTER 6

If Captain Gallcob was surprised when his aspirant passenger suddenly produced a ship-stone and ordered him to set sail, he did not show it. Instead, he simply nodded and started shouting orders to his crew. Maena thought she even detected a hint of relief in the captain's manner. She didn't blame him. A long sea voyage with a ship full of redcaps was a thoroughly awful prospect.

Maena rested her arms on the ship's hand-rail and watched the slowly receding quayside as they pulled away. She spotted one of King Oberon's redcaps talking animatedly to the harbour master and pointing at the Regal Dolphin as its sails billowed, catching the wind. The redcap and the dwarves on shore jogged down the pier to another ship, the Conclave, and hurried up the gangplank. Maena could just make out the orders being shouted on board the Conclave as its sails were unfurled and the anchor pulled up from the bottom of the harbour.

The Regal Dolphin was already passing the two forts that guarded the harbour entrance before the Conclave had started moving. Maena breathed a sigh of relief when the lone sentry on the battlements gave them a friendly wave.

'We are really leaving,' said Neave.

Maena had not noticed the aspirant come and stand next to her.

'Yes, we are,' said Maena.

'*Neave is not going back to the farm. You lied.*' Hevac's voice sounded sullen in her head.

'I did,' said Maena.

'Did what?' asked Neave.

'It doesn't matter,' said Maena.

'*Yes, it does!*'

Hevac was getting on her nerves. The sooner she could get out of this vessel and leave him to it the better.

'*Something I can agree with.*'

Once they were clear of the harbour entrance and heading for the open sea, the Conclave continued to pursue the Regal Dolphin. This surprised Maena as, if they did not have a ship-stone, they risked the wrath of Saltrock's guardians: the giant squid. She and her sisters had grown the beasts using blood magic to keep unwanted shipping away from the shores of Saltrock. Unless you had a ship-stone, your boat would be in danger of being turned into a slowly sinking collection of damp firewood.

Captain Gallcob joined them at the rear of the ship. He muttered to himself as he pulled out a brass spyglass from a battered leather case and extended it.

'They don't have a ship-stone. Why aren't they turning back?' asked Neave.

Captain Gallcob focussed the spyglass on their pursuers. 'It's the damned redcaps.' He slammed the spyglass shut. 'They're forcing old Redrock to follow us.'

'Forcing?' queried Neave.

'Looks like they've got a blade on him.'

'Won't the crew stop them?' asked Neave.

'Not unless they know they don't have a ship-stone,' said Maena.

'Your servant is right,' said Captain Gallcob. 'The poor bastards will just assume they have a stone.'

'*We need to warn them.*'

Maena knew that wasn't going to happen. Getting close enough to warn them would be getting close enough to be attacked.

'Oh well. Better them than us,' said Maena.

'Your servant is right again,' said Captain Gallcob.

She was getting tired of being called a servant.

'*It's only been two days. Try it your whole life.*'

'We should at least pick up survivors,' said Neave.

Maena sighed. 'And what if some of them are redcaps?'

Neave was silent.

Captain Gallcob coughed. 'I'd rather not have any of those little buggers on board my ship. Begging your pardon, aspirant.'

Distant shouts of alarm from the pursuing ship interrupted their deliberations.

Captain Gallcob raised his spyglass. 'Gods. I can see tentacles.'

'Where?' asked Neave leaning forward as if this would improve her view.

Captain Gallcob lowered the spyglass and pointed. 'There.'

Maena followed the line of his finger and saw a pair of huge grey tentacles slowly rising from the waves next to the Conclave.

'That's sorted then,' said Maena.

'*Sorted?*' The internal voice sounded horrified.

'Sorted?' asked Neave. Although her question echoed her brother's, she sounded more curious than horrified.

'Unless they have a practitioner of blood magic on board, the guardian will finish them,' said Maena.

Maena saw Captain Gallcob look from her to Neave and back again, an appraising look on his face. She realised she was sounding quite knowledgeable for a servant that smells faintly of goat. 'That's what you told me, aspirant.'

'Oh. Right,' said Neave.

The distant shouts of panic on board the other ship were joined by distant screams as the tentacles started sweeping across the deck, smashing the main mast in two and sending several of the crew into the water.

'See? Sorted,' said Maena.

'Your servant is both practical and callous, aspirant,' said Captain Gallcob.

Neave didn't respond. Maena saw that she was watching the Conclave being turned into matchwood by several of the massive grey tentacles.

'*It's horrible.*'

Maena leaned in close to Neave and whispered, 'I am sorry. It is necessary.'

The peculiar thing was that Maena actually felt a small pang of sorrow for the sailors and their families. She shook her head trying to clear her head of the unfamiliar feelings.

'*Perhaps there is some good in you after all.*'

As she listened to the distant crashing of wood and dying screams, Maena wondered at her reaction. It must be something to do with this vessel. She surreptitiously looked down at her body. Maybe it wasn't just the big hands, excessive hair and extra appendage she was having trouble getting used to. With a quiet sigh, she left the others watching the fragments of sinking ship and went to find somewhere to have a bit of a lie down.

CHAPTER 7

The hustle and bustle of the Aston streets swept around John and Julienne as they made their way to the docks. The crowds got thicker as they approached the quayside and John was obliged to play up the violent side of his mercenary persona to force their way through the crowd.

'Busy down here,' he remarked to Julienne.

Julienne was holding his hand as they worked their way to the ship they had booked passage on. 'It always is. Keep your eyes open and one hand on your purse. The local pickpockets won't normally try to rob a man of war such as yourself, but no sense taking any chances.'

They managed to make it to their destination without being robbed and saw the gangplank was down allowing access to the ship from the jetty.

As they stepped onto the deck of the ship, a familiar bellowing voice greeted them. 'Welcome aboard!'

'Captain Pollow. Good to see you again,' said Julienne.

Apart from a spanking new mast, the Banshee looked much as it had on their previous voyage beyond the Sunset Isles. Captain Pollow's beard had, if anything, grown even more heroic since they had last seen him.

'And good to see you lass.' Captain Pollow made a show of

peering around behind John and Julienne. 'None of the short folk in tow this time I see.'

'Just the two of us on this trip,' said John.

'You've got the same cabins. Jimmy here can stow your gear for you.' Captain Pollow nodded towards a familiar faced member of the crew.

'Alright, John,' said Jimmy as he took John's pack.

'Hello, Jimmy,' said John.

'We just need the one cabin,' said Julienne.

Jimmy coughed and covered his mouth.

Captain Pollow's eyebrows rose a little, and he winked at John before frowning slightly. 'I hope you don't expect a discount?'

'Of course not. You will be paid the agreed amount.' Julienne turned to smile at a smirking Jimmy. 'Take our things to the fore-cabin if you don't mind.'

The crewman tugged a forelock and hurried off with their bags.

'As the renowned mercenary John's servant. I will be sleeping at the foot of his bed.' Julienne dropped into a shallow curtsy.

'Renowned is he? Can't say as I've ever heard of him.'

'I'm sure you and the crew can make sure he is known in the taverns and opium dens of Olong when we arrive,' said Julienne.

'Me and the lads can spread a good rumour, that's for sure. There will be an additional fee to pay,' said Captain Pollow.

'I never expected anything different, Captain.'

* * *

By the second day, John had rediscovered his sea-legs. The first day had been pretty miserable. The weather had taken a turn for the worse soon after they left Aston and his inner ear had taken a while to adjust. Julienne, on the other hand, had been relentlessly cheerful and spent her day talking to the crew. John supposed she was gathering information to report back to Luke, Lord Rychard's chief spymaster.

The two of them spent the voyage practicing their roles, and by the fourth day John was more comfortable playing the part of a hardened mercenary. In fact, he was quite enjoying it. The crew played along and everyone had great fun making up the exploits of John 'Quickblade' Horner. He wasn't sure about 'Quickblade'. Although he was a competent swordsman, he might have trouble living up to the skill promised by the nickname bestowed on his alter-ego by the crew of the Banshee.

John and Julienne were enjoying some private time in their cabin when a commotion started on board the Banshee. He could hear the footsteps of the crew moving swiftly around the ship and Captain Pollow's voice could be heard shouting orders. Julienne stopped what she was doing when the deck noticeably tilted as the Banshee changed course.

'We shouldn't be changing course now.' Julienne looked up at him from under her tousled blond hair. 'We should find out what's happening.'

'Maybe in a minute?' asked John hopefully.

'Sorry, lover boy.' Julienne levered herself up onto her forearms and then pushed herself up onto her feet. 'Wear your sword belt. I have a feeling it could be trouble.'

When the two of them had dressed and made it onto the deck, it was apparent what was causing the commotion. An oared galley was bearing down on them and Captain Pollow had ordered the course change to avoid them. It did not look like it was working. If there was enough wind, the Banshee would have left the other ship standing, but the winds were light.

'Who are they Captain?' asked John.

'Illian Reavers, curse our luck.'

'What are they doing so far north?' asked Julienne.

'Does it matter? They're here and we had better get ready to make a fight of it,' said Captain Pollow.

'Can we not just give them our cargo?' asked John.

'Aye, but they'd more than likely take it, sink the Banshee and sell us into slavery,' said Captain Pollow.

'Fight it is,' said John. He put his hand on the hilt of his sword. Maybe he could live up to the stories of John 'Quickblade' Horner.

'Get ready, lads. You know reavers. If they capture you alive, you'll be their cabin plaything for the trip to the slave market. I say, we don't let them capture us.'

There was silence from the crew who clutched their weapons tightly and looked pensively at the galley bearing down on them.

Jimmy held his cutlass defiantly aloft. 'They'll not take the Banshee Cap'n.' He turned to the rest of the crew. 'We've had worse! Remember that tentacled horror? This lot will be easy.' He made a rude gesture at the approaching vessel.

John hoped that Jimmy was right. The galley was getting closer and he could see some reavers armed with bows taking position on the prow of the oncoming ship. They started firing before they were really in range, the feathered shafts plunging into the grey sea.

'Hold your fire!' shouted Captain Pollow, holding his cutlass aloft.

Half the crew had armed themselves with crossbows and were taking aim as best they could while the deck pitched and rolled beneath them. They'd be lucky to hit anyone thought John. But, on the bright side, the Illian archers would also need a healthy dose of luck to hit any of the Banshee's crew.

Captain Pollow slashed his cutlass downwards. 'Fire!'

The crew started to fire their crossbows.

Most of the bolts went wide or thumped into the prow of the oncoming galley. Then, a cheer went up as one of the Illians was swept from his perch. John wasn't surprised that it was Julienne's shot that had managed to find its mark. She was a scarily good shot with the weapon.

John drew his sword and was reassured by the feel of the worn grip in his hand. 'Here they come.'

Julienne didn't reply. She just carefully placed her crossbow on the deck and drew her own sword.

The sound of the galley's oars biting into the water and the curses and war-cries of the reavers grew closer and louder until, with a crash, the iron shod ram impacted the Banshee. Several reavers leapt onto the deck of the Banshee, curved scimitars in their hands and murder in their eyes.

'No bugger's taking our ship! Gut them lads!' bellowed Captain Pollow.

A wild eyed reaver charged at John screaming words in the harsh tongue of Illia. John used his sword to deflect the wicked blade and then stepped to one side, following up with a swing of his own that cut deeply into the man's midriff.

John left the reaver lying in a growing pool of blood and looked for another target. There was plenty of choice. Two of the Banshee's crew were down, felled in the initial savagery of the attack. Half a dozen lifeless Illian's also littered the deck, and the wood was becoming slippery with blood.

His blood ran cold as he heard a familiar voice cry out in pain. He looked to his left and saw Julienne facing off against a massive Illian. The man was seven feet tall and wielded a massive wooden cudgel in one hand and a long length of chain in the other. This chain was wrapped around Julienne's sword arm and, with a wicked grin, the man pulled on the chain jerking her into reach of his club.

John didn't hesitate. He launched himself at Julienne's assailant and grabbed the man's arm preventing him from bringing the club into contact with her. The Illian grunted and tried to shake John loose. He grimly held on as he was flailed about like a rag doll until the reaver let go of the chain and smashed his massive fist into the side of John's head.

John couldn't help letting go, his head spinning from the impact. He fell to the deck and groggily tried to stand up, but the combination of the blow and the movement of the deck kept him on his hands and knees looking at the floor.

He heard a grunt of pain. This time it wasn't Julienne. John heard the thump of something heavy hitting the deck beside him and lifted his head to meet the dead, wide-eyed stare of the fallen reaver. Then, Julienne hooked her arms under John's armpits and hauled him to his feet.

'Are you ok?'

Julienne flexed her arm experimentally. 'Nothing broken.'

Any further diagnosis of Julienne's injuries was cut short by two more reavers heading their way. John and Julienne moved into a combat ready position, swords raised, instinctively standing so that they covered and supported each other.

He concentrated on the reaver in front of him, confident that Julienne could take care of herself. John saw his opponent look down at the lifeless bodies of the reavers at their feet and slow his approach.

John beckoned his opponent, inviting him to attack. 'Come on then, you bastard.'

When the man did not react, John tried again. 'You fight like a girl.'

'Hey! I heard that,' said Julienne. There was a ring of steel on steel as she parried a blow aimed at her head.

The man in front of John glanced over at Julienne. John, seizing on this momentary distraction, stepped forward into a lunge aimed at the man's exposed left side. The reaver reacted a moment too late and John's blade opened a vicious cut across his ribs.

The reaver put his hand to his wound and it came away smeared in blood. John attempted to press his advantage with an overhead swing but his opponent managed to raise his scimitar and block the attack, sliding the force of John's blow to one side. The reaver then lashed out with his foot. John cried out in pain as it connected with his knee making his leg give way. He desperately scrambled to bring his sword up to meet the inevitable follow-up blow and the ring of metal on metal greeted his success. He did not have time to counter-attack and was forced to hold his sword in place as the reaver hammered downwards again, trying to use brute force to break John's guard.

The muscles in John's arm screamed with fatigue and he braced it with his other arm as another blow struck his sword, now inches above his head. Desperately, he kicked upwards towards the man's groin and was rewarded by a gasp of pain as his assailant staggered backwards cursing in his strange tongue.

John got to his feet and readied himself; the reaver had mostly recovered from the kick to his testicles and was now glaring at him with murderous eyes.

John brought his sword up to a guard position and saw the Illian's scowl change into a wide, gap-toothed grin. He was momentarily confused, then his world exploded as something hit the back of his head and everything went black.

CHAPTER 8

The back of John's head hurt, filling his world with a dull throb of pain. Slowly, he became aware of his surroundings. He was lying on a wooden floor. He could feel the rough texture of the planking. The floor was also moving. He was momentarily worried that this was caused by his head injury, then he remembered that he was on a ship. He cracked open an eyelid. It was dark. Unable to see anything, he concentrated on what he could hear. The wooden creaking of the ship and the sound of somebody breathing nearby. Peering in the direction of the breathing, he could just make out the dark shape of someone sitting against the bulkhead. He was not alone.

'Julienne?' he asked hopefully. His voice was dry and cracked.

'It's me, Jimmy. Sorry, mate.'

'Jimmy?'

'Yeah. Just you and me down here.'

'Where is down here?' John wasn't sure he would like the answer to this one.

'The reaver's ship.'

He was right. He didn't like that answer. 'Where are the others?'

'Dead, mostly. Peter and Hez got put on the oars I think. Captain's dead.'

'What about Julienne?' asked John.

It was hard to tell in the gloom, but he got the impression Jimmy was looking at the floor. 'She. Ah.'

'What? What's happened?'

'She's...'

'Gods sake, Jimmy, tell me.'

'John, the captain had her taken somewhere. I don't know.'

'You don't know?'

'I only know a few words of Illian, and none of them wanted a beer or a prostitute.'

It wasn't the first time Julienne had disappeared to an unknown fate. But this time seemed different. She was skilled and resourceful, but what could she do against a boat full of Illian reavers?

'Uh, I'm sure she's fine.' Jimmy did not sound convincing.

John attempted to sit up, felt dizzy and lay back down again. 'Shit.'

'Glad you're awake though,' said Jimmy.

John didn't reply as he waited for the dancing spots of light to fade.

'Was worried you weren't going to wake up,' said Jimmy.

John tried sitting up again. This time he managed to stay up.

Jimmy sniffed. 'What are we going to do, John?'

'I don't know. We're not in chains, that's good.'

'Yeah. I guess we've nowhere to go even if we got through the door,' said Jimmy.

John's stomach rumbled loudly.

'They brought us some food earlier. Pretty sure they'll feed us soon,' said Jimmy.

'Why so sure?'

'We're merchandise.'

'Merchandise?'

Jimmy let out a short hollow laugh. 'We're going to Olong all right. Just to the slave market instead of the taverns.'

John groaned. The full reality of their situation hitting him. 'We're so screwed.'

'I hear it's not a bad life. If you get a good master,' said Jimmy.

'We should try to overpower the guard when he comes with the food,' said John.

'Not as easy as you make it sound. He's big, and has a big stick.'

'You know what they say: the bigger they are the harder they fall.'

'Whoever said that wasn't stuck in the slave pen on an Illian reaver ship,' said Jimmy.

Their discussion was interrupted by the rattle of a key in the door's lock.

'Now's our chance,' said John.

'I still think this is a bad idea,' said Jimmy.

The door opened to reveal the silhouette of a muscular, broad-shouldered man. He had a large cudgel tucked into a wide leather belt and carried a wooden bowl. The man ducked as he entered, said something unintelligible, and placed the bowl on the floor by the door before turning to leave.

John lunged forwards for the bowl, quickly picked it up and threw it at their captor. The brown sludge it contained splattered across the man's back and the bowl glanced off his arm and hit the wall.

John followed up this culinary attack with a low tackle,

launching himself at the larger man and wrapping his arms around his thick waist. He could smell the spicy sludge as he hung on, trying to bring the man down. His right arm was pinning the cudgel in place and he felt the man tug on it twice before giving up and smashing a big ham-fist down on to the top of his head. His head ringing from this attack, John doggedly hung on as the fist came down a second time, this time onto his arm. The shock of the blow loosened his grip so that he fell to the floor.

John groggily looked up and saw the man's foot coming down towards his face. He rolled to the left, but the boot grazed the back of his head where he had been hit earlier lighting his head up with an explosion of pain. A kick in the stomach compounded his misery, and he lay gasping on the floor. From this vantage point he saw Jimmy spring up at their captor and out of his field of vision. He then heard a meaty thump and Jimmy flew back into view, slamming into the bulkhead before dropping to the floor unconscious. Jimmy had been right. This had been a bad idea.

John was hoisted onto his feet and the reaver shouted something at him, warm spittle and bad breath landing on his cheek. He tried a shrug, but that only made his ribs hurt.

Then he was dragged out and up on to the deck. Here, he was tied to a mast, his arms hugging it. There was more jabbering in the foreign language and then John felt a line of fire across his back. The third lash with the whip sent his head flopping forwards as he slipped into the relief of unconsciousness.

CHAPTER 9

The two dwarves had misjudged their travel time slightly and were walking the final leg of their journey by moonlight. The narrow trail was well lit by the full moon which meant they did not need to use a lantern to light their way. This was fortunate, as a lantern was more likely to attract any trolls who happened to be hunting nearby. Bienia remembered her last encounter with a troll. It was not one she wished to repeat.

'There it is,' said Brynhild.

A stone hut was huddled in the valley, sheltered from the cold wind blowing over the rocks and wild grass of the Troll Fells. This was the hut of Brynhild's uncle Snorri. She and her cousins had built it for him after he returned from an expedition to the Spiky mountains where he had encountered the mystics who dwelt there. It was the mystics that had apparently shown him the 'secrets of the universe'. Brynhild had told Bienia that she and her cousins suspected his spiritual enlightenment had more to do with the mystic's mushroom tea than any real insight into the workings of reality.

Ten minutes later they were outside the hut. A flickering warm glow of light leaked out from behind the shutters and under the door. Brynhild knocked on the door and Bienia heard the scraping of a chair across wooden floorboards followed by the clatter of multiple bolts being pulled back.

Then, the door opened a crack and the occupant of the hut peered out into the night. 'Who's that? Come on, speak up.'

'It's us uncle. Brynhild and Bienia,' said Brynhild.

The door was flung open to reveal Snorri. His beard seemed wilder than ever and his eyes gleamed with pleasure. 'Girls! Come in, come in.'

Pockle the fairy poked his head out of Brynhild's backpack. 'How the feck are you, you old bugger?'

Snorri smiled. 'And Pockle, of course.' He moved to one side and beckoned them into the hut.

Bienia was grateful to sit down in front of the fireplace. She took off her boots and wiggled her toes experimentally.

'Thank the gods. They still work.'

Snorri raised a bushy eyebrow. 'Losing the love of marching lass?'

'Not sure I'd have ever described it as love exactly. It's just a way of getting from here to there,' said Bienia.

'Or there to here. Get the tea on, uncle,' said Brynhild.

'Better to fecking fly,' said Pockle.

'For once, I think I agree with Pockle,' said Bienia.

Snorri smiled to himself as he listened to the conversation. He hung the kettle over the fire then sat down, the three of them forming a cosy semicircle around its bright and cheery warmth.

'So, how did things go with the High Queen?' asked Snorri.

'You haven't heard?' asked Bienia.

'Of course he fecking hasn't,' said Pockle. 'Neither would you living out here in the arse end of nowhere.'

'I am well aware of recent events, and am making polite

conversation. Something Pockle has never got the hang of.' Snorri was still smiling despite his admonishing tone.

'Blow it out your arse you old git,' said Pockle.

Snorri kept smiling. 'It is wonderful to see you as well, old friend.'

'Got any of your blackberry wine?' asked the fairy.

Snorri nodded amiably and retrieved a dark green bottle from a cupboard.

'Last years vintage.' Snorri blew the dust from the neck of the bottle.

'Does that make it any better?' asked Bienia.

'I suppose you could describe it as slightly more drinkable than the stuff he's made with this year's berry crop,' said Brynhild.

Snorri chuckled as he pulled the stopper out of the bottle with a satisfying pop. He offered the bottle to the two shieldmaidens.

'I'll pass,' said Brynhild.

Bienia shook her head. It had been a long day, she would probably sleep better without Snorri's dubious brew.

Pockle, on the other hand, greedily accepted a thimbleful of the dark red liquid. 'This stuff is great. Really gets you shitfaced.'

'What brings you out here to visit your uncle?' asked Snorri.

Brynhild took a sip of her tea before answering. 'It's sort of on the way to Ironhome. Plus, I think this one has paid his debt to you.' She nodded at the fairy.

'I have?' asked Pockle.

'Ah yes, the defeat of the Clans. Caused quite a stir back in the Silver Hills,' said Snorri.

'I suppose it would,' said Bienia. She wondered if anyone would hold it against her if they found out she'd been the one to kill the High Queen. Not kill, she mentally corrected, evict. High Queen Maena had turned out to be something called a svalfae, able to transfer her consciousness from one vessel to another, and had ended up in Bienia's head for a year. It was odd, she reflected, that she almost missed Maena's acerbic commentary on her daily life.

Snorri pulled a clay pipe and leather tobacco pouch from a pocket. 'I don't think the Hammerfist are going to forgive the Ironfist for a while.'

'They took it badly?' asked Bienia.

'Old King Sigfrid didn't want them to make a fuss, so they voted him out and installed Ragnar Hammerfist as their King.'

'Sigfrid's not High King any more?'

'Technically yes, but he's not King of the Hammerfist. I have to admit I don't really understand the politics of it.' He pulled a stick with one end glowing red hot from the fire, held it to the bowl of his pipe, and puffed furiously to get the tobacco lit. 'That's one of the reasons I moved out here. Can't abide politics.'

'Ragnar Hammerfist,' said Brynhild. 'Is that Ragnar "The Hammer of Retribution" Hammerfist?'

'Well, that's just great,' said Bienia. She had been part of a joint Ironfist and Hammerfist expeditionary force raiding deep into ice goblin territory. An attempt by Old King Sigfrid at reconciliation between the rival clans. The Hammerfist contingent had been led by Ragnar and the whole thing had degenerated into a brawl between Ironfist and Hammerfist. If he was now leading the Hammerfist, it was only a matter of time before hostilities broke out.

'Hostilities have already broken out,' said Snorri.

'Perfect,' said Bienia.

'Sounds like it's all fecking kicking off,' said Pockle. 'I guess you two broads will need me to watch out for you if you're heading into the middle of a sodding dwarven feud.'

'But your debt is paid. You can return to hanging around here drinking all my booze,' said Snorri.

'Sorry, fella. Me and Bryn are tight as. Where she goes, I go.' Pockle fluttered up, perched on Brynhild's shoulder and put his hand on her head.

'I see.' Snorri puffed on his pipe and blew a contemplative smoke-ring.

Was Bienia imagining things, or was Bryn blushing?

Bienia coughed. 'Anyway. Is it alright if we stay a while before we leave for Ironhome?'

'Of course,' said Snorri.

CHAPTER 10

Ironhome. Although Bienia was in service to the King of Asterland, Maena knew that the shieldmaiden had planned to return here for a while. Maena had never visited the home of the Ironfist during her tenure as High Queen of the clans, but returning to the Silver Hills made her feel nostalgic.

She looked down at her hands, gripping the handrail of the Lake Ferrum ferry. They were larger and more calloused than any of her previous vessels' hands, and she was still not used to the hair.

'*Nothing wrong with my hands. They are honest hands.*'

Goatherd's hands. Honestly.

'*They are not yours. I was quite happy being alone with my hands.*'

Maena was aware of what being alone with his hands could mean for Hevac. She had experimented once during a quiet time alone on board the ship. It had been an unsettling experience for both of them.

'*Unsettling is a bit of an understatement.*'

Maena put the incident from her mind and looked towards Ironhome. Small boats dotted the shore of the lake, watched over by the simple cottages of the fishermen. Nets and crab pots were piled in untidy heaps next to the boats. Looking past the cottages, her eye was drawn to the stone walls of Ironhome fortress which was constructed from massive blocks of granite, hewn from the mountains and put together here, on the shore of Lake Ferrum.

'It's quite impressive,' said Neave.

Maena looked sidelong at the aspirant. She had almost forgotten she was there.

'Mistress—' Neave checked herself. 'Hevac. I am still concerned about seeking Bienia's help.'

'Don't be,' said Maena.

'But—'

'Neave. It is not your place to think about these things.'

Neave fell silent, then looked towards Ironhome, a troubled look on her face.

'Neave, you are my most faithful companion. I will be relying on you to watch my back while we are among the Ironfist dwarves.'

Neave's face went from troubled to resolute. 'Your wish is my will, mistress.'

Maena was momentarily taken aback by her use of the old fey-folk phrase but she was glad to have focussed Neave's mind. 'Remember that the Ironfist dwarves will not show any deference to you because you are an aspirant. They do not know what an aspirant is.'

'So ignorant,' said Neave.

The ferry forged on, sliding over the wide still waters of the lake. The lake was huge, and the far shore became an indistinct smudge in the distance as they got closer to Ironhome, passing dwarves hauling nets full of jumping silver fish out of the lake and onto their boats.

It wasn't long before the ferry arrived at their destination and moored alongside a weathered wooden jetty. They disembarked and made their way along the jetty to the shore. The smell of fresh-caught fish was strong and the hollers and calls of working dwarves surrounded them. They walked past the cottages near the shore and followed a cobbled road towards the center of Ironhome. Maena knew the Ironfist shieldmaidens had a great wooden hall in Ironhome and hoped to find Bienia there.

The gate was open, and they joined the steady stream of dwarves entering and leaving the fortress. The guards on the gate paid them little heed as they emerged from the gatehouse into a massive courtyard. There were many buildings around the walls, and the space in the middle was filled with a bustling market; the hubbub of the market's patrons and the cries of the sellers echoed off the fortress walls

Maena approached the nearest stall. It was covered in glass jars.

'Pickled eel, sir?' asked the stall-holder.

'*I do not like eels.*'

Maena agreed with Hevac. Besides, she was not here to buy snacks. 'No. Can you tell me where the shieldmaidens' hall is?'

'Over there.' The dwarf pointed. 'It would be polite to buy some eels, you know.'

Maena ignored him and headed towards the indicated building. It was of wooden construction, and the lintel of the main door was decorated with brightly painted round shields.

The noisy clamour of the market faded as they walked inside. A long table ran down the middle of the hall; smoke was rising from a large fire pit at the far end of the hall and mostly out of a hole in the roof. Enough of the smoke did not escape to make the interior of the hall smell of bonfire. Half a dozen female dwarves were sitting at the end of the table nearest the fire. One of them looked up as Maena and Neave walked the length of the table towards them.

'Greetings. My name is Hevac, and this is my sister, Neave.'

The shieldmaiden puffed on her clay pipe and blew a large lazy smoke ring before speaking. 'Greetings. I am Freya of the clan Ironfist. What is your clan Hevac and Neave?'

'Saltrock,' said Maena. She didn't see much point in trying to lie.

'Wasn't that the High Queen's clan?' asked one of the other dwarves at the table.

'Who is the High Queen?' Maena asked innocently. She exchanged a look with Neave, willing the aspirant to remain silent.

'Della is right. The High Queen was from Saltrock.' Freya sucked on her pipe and released a billowing cloud of smoke towards the ceiling. 'So, what can we do for you, Hevac of clan Saltrock?'

'I seek my friend, the shieldmaiden Bienia,' said Maena.

Freya coughed in surprise. 'You know Bienia, but don't know about her killing the High Queen?'

'Oh, *that* High Queen. We don't like to talk about her on Saltrock,' said Maena.

'I see,' said Freya.

'So. Bienia?'

'I don't like this. He's from Saltrock,' said Della.

Freya nodded. 'How do we know we can trust you, Hevac of Saltrock?'

Maena stroked her beard thoughtfully; she was starting to get used to having facial hair. Knowing what she did of these dwarves and Bienia, how could she earn their trust? Then she knew. Smiling, she drew a single gold coin from a belt pouch and held it up so it glinted. 'I have a gold coin which says I can out drink any one of you.'

Freya's eyes lit up. 'Oh ho! A challenge.'

'You get the coin if I lose. If I win, you tell me where I can find Bienia,' said Maena.

'*Wait! I can't drink that much ale!*' Hevac's panicked voice sounded in her head.

'Let me, Freya,' said Della. 'I'll put this Saltrock idiot in his place.'

Freya stood up and went to the wall where a pair of yard beer glasses were hanging. The glasses were shaped with a bulb at one end and a widening stem. 'Siggi, fetch a barrel of ale.'

A dark haired shieldmaiden, who had been sitting watching the conversation silently, nodded, went to a stack of kegs at the back of the hall and selected one.

Maena shuffled behind Neave and whispered in her ear, 'Hand.'

Neave kept her body between her and the others and held her right hand behind her back. Maena drew her dagger and pricked the end of Neave's finger. She then smeared the blood welling out of the cut across the blade and whispered some ancient words of power before wiping the blade clean on the back of Neave's tunic and then replacing it in its sheath.

Neave sucked the cut on her finger while Freya held a yard between her legs and carefully poured ale from the small keg into the wide top.

The other dwarves had started making side bets on the outcome. One of the shieldmaidens winked suggestively at Maena.

Della cracked her knuckles and took the first yard to be filled.

Neave watched on, a vague look of concern on her face as Freya topped off the second yard of ale and handed it to Maena.

'Ready?' asked Freya.

'I am,' said Maena.

Della nodded.

Freya clapped her hands. 'Drink!'

'*Oh no...*'

Maena raised her glass, closed her eyes, and started to gulp down the bitter tasting ale. With the aid of the blood magic it was easy. Her throat relaxed, opened, and the ale poured down, filling her belly with swirling liquid. The enchantment was an old one used during hedonistic revels to keep a clear head while giving the appearance of full participation. Her glass was empty in a matter of seconds and she heard gasps of astonishment from the other dwarves. She opened her eyes to see a wide eyed Della only halfway through her yard.

Freya shook her head in wonder. 'Well, I'll be...'

Maena belched. She could taste beer on the ejected gas.

'*How embarrassing.*'

'Damn it Helga,' said Freya.

Helga, the shieldmaiden that had winked at Maena, whooped and started collecting her winnings. Apparently, she was the only one who had bet on the strange male dwarf from Saltrock.

'Now. Bienia,' said Maena.

Freya shook her head. 'She is not here.'

'What?'

'I said she's not here.'

'I thought that's what you said. Why did I just drink that yard of ale?'

Freya shrugged. 'Seemed like a fun idea.'

'It was a great idea,' said Helga as she counted out stacks of silver coins while her compatriots looked on glumly.

'So, you can't help me at all?' asked Maena.

'Didn't say that.'

Maena was starting to lose patience with this annoying dwarf, Freya. 'Do you know where I might find her?'

'You could try Snorri's place, in the Troll Fells. That's if she isn't in Asterland still,' said Freya.

'Who is Snorri?' asked Neave.

'He's Brynhild's uncle,' said Maena. This could be good news. She remembered Bienia and Brynhild talking about this uncle. Apparently, he knew a thing or two about the fey-folk. He may be able to help.

'Bienia may be at his place with Brynhild. It's on the way to Asterland,' said Freya.

'You could have led with that,' said Maena.

Freya just shrugged again, grinned and then took a deep pull on her pipe before blowing a wobbly smoke ring towards Maena and Neava.

Maena coughed and tried to wave the smoke away. 'Do you have a map?'

'Della, get a map for Hevac,' said Freya.

'What?' Della put her hands on her hips and glared at Freya.

'You lost, so you get to buy a map in the market.'

Della shot Maena and Neave a dark look before she left the hall in search of a map.

'Why are you looking for Bienia?' Freya leaned back in her chair with her hands behind her head and pipe stem clenched between her teeth.

'None of your business,' said Maena.

'Are you, ah, friendly with Bienia?' asked Helga.

The look Helga was giving Maena could only be described as 'hungry'.

'*I'm not sure I like that look.*'

'Not exclusively.' Maena smiled at the young shieldmaiden.

'*Wait a minute, I don't want you using my body for anything carnal.*'

'Are you and your sister staying long?' Helga sounded hopeful.

Maena shook her head. 'No. We get the map, and we go.'

'*Thank the gods for that.*'

'Oh.' Helga looked a little crestfallen.

CHAPTER 11

The sound of the axe hitting logs was loud in the morning air. Bienia stopped for a moment and wiped her brow. It was actually good to do some manual work. She hadn't chopped firewood since she was a young dwarf growing up near Ironhome. She had forgotten the simple pleasure that could be taken in splitting the wood along the grain.

Snorri and Brynhild had gone to check the snares the old dwarf had previously set. Hopefully, they would all be eating a nice rabbit stew for lunch. Apart from Pockle, who would be eating raw rabbit.

'You look good out of your armour.'

Bienia turned in the direction of the voice and almost dropped her axe. 'Hevac. What in the nine hells are you doing here?'

The goatherd was standing next to the corner of the cabin. He let out a small gasp and put his hand on the wall before answering, 'I've come to see you, obviously.'

A second newcomer came around the corner of the cabin and waved. 'Hello, Bienia,' said Neave.

'Your sister too?' To say that Bienia was surprised was an understatement.

'We had to, ah, leave in a hurry,' said Hevac.

'But why? You have the farm to run. Don't you?'

'Please. A bunch of smelly goats? What would I want with that?' Hevac wrinkled his nose in a very un-Hevac-like expression of disgust.

'Are you feeling alright? Neave, is your brother okay?' asked Bienia.

'My brother is...not himself,' said Neave.

'Why, what's wrong with him?' asked Bienia.

'Sorry. What is happening on Saltrock is distressing me. I need your help,' said Hevac.

'It must be serious for you to give up the farm, you had better come inside.'

Maena was feeling disorientated. The rush of feelings she had felt when she first saw the shieldmaiden chopping wood with her shirt sleeves rolled up and her bare arms clearly visible was unsettling. When Bienia had turned to face Maena, the sight of her unbuttoned shirt had nearly finished her. She had occupied male vessels before, but never one with a subordinate personality still intact. She was finding his influence tedious.

'*I am right here you know.*'

How could she forget? She felt the urge to rut intensely. This was something she had never contemplated with the shieldmaiden before taking this vessel. Maybe coming to Bienia for help had been a bad idea.

'*A bit late to think of that now. Anyway, I am glad we came.*'

Hevac was right. She had cast her lot, now she had to see things through.

* * *

Bienia, Neave and Hevac were all seated at the table in Snorri's cabin. Each of them had a gently steaming cup of tea in front of them.

Bienia massaged her temples. 'So, let me get this straight. Oberon, the King of the fey-folk that Pockle goes on about, is on Saltrock preparing for an invasion of the mainland.'

Hevac nodded. 'Right.'

'And you want Snorri to help you deal with him?'

'Again, correct.'

'What makes you think Snorri can help?'

'From what you told me, he knows about the fey-folk.'

Bienia didn't remember telling Hevac about Snorri. 'When did I tell you about him?'

Hevac shifted in his seat, looking away from Bienia. 'When we travelled to Andraste's house.'

'Did I? Strange, I don't remember.'

'We talked of many things,' said Hevac.

Bienia didn't remember it like that. Hevac was more the strong silent type. Still, maybe she had talked to him about Snorri, how else would Hevac know about him?

Hevac interrupted her train of thought. 'You could also help, Bienia.'

'Me? What makes you say that?'

Hevac was silent a moment. 'You successfully ended Andraste.'

'So I did. What about Maena, what is she doing?'

Bienia didn't miss Neave start a little at the mention of Maena.

'She is in hiding,' said Hevac.

'Where?' asked Bienia.

Neave looked at Hevac, then back to Bienia, and then sipped her tea.

'That's not important,' said Hevac.

Bienia held Hevac's gaze for a few seconds. 'It isn't?'

The seconds stretched toward a minute.

'No,' said Hevac.

'Neave, can Hevac and I have a moment alone please?' asked Bienia.

Neave looked to Hevac who nodded.

'I will be outside,' said Neave.

Once she was gone, Bienia rounded on Hevac. 'Now that she has gone, you can tell me where Maena is.'

'No, I cannot,' said Hevac.

Bienia was dumbfounded. 'Hevac. You can tell me. You know you can trust me.'

'Nevertheless, I will not be telling you.'

She got to her feet, strode over to Hevac, grabbed his chin and looked into his eyes. 'What's the matter, Hevac?'

Hevac knocked her hand away. 'Nothing. I just need your help to deal with Oberon. Is that so hard to understand?'

'To be quite honest, yes. Why the sudden interest in something that isn't a goat farm or related to you?'

Hevac stood and took Bienia's hand. 'Maybe I have worked out what is important.'

Bienia said nothing. The thrill of their hands touching sent her pulse racing.

Hevac reached up and gently stroked Bienia's cheek. 'You are magnificent.'

Bienia moaned gently and pulled Hevac close, her mouth greedily meeting his. At first he responded but then, without warning, he broke away, pushing Bicnia away from him.

'What's the matter?' asked Bienia.

'Nothing, it's just. I can't do this right now. Not until Oberon is defeated.'

'I understand,' said Bienia. She didn't, but Hevac seemed distressed and she didn't want to upset him any further.

'Thankyou.' Hevac straightened his shoulders. 'Nothing is more important than stopping Oberon.'

'I suppose you are right,' said Bienia.

'Of course I am. Now, if you'll excuse me, I think I will go and talk with my sister.'

'Sure. Just be ready to repeat everything you told me when the others get back.'

Hevac nodded. 'Of course, Bienia.'

Maena closed the cabin door behind her and drew a deep shuddering breath. She had nearly lost control back there. She couldn't trust this vessel around Bienia, its feelings were too deep rooted for her to suppress.

'*It? I have a name.*'

'Calm yourself.' This was meant for herself as much as Hevac.

She took a few steadying deep breaths, straightened her clothes, and then noticed Neave watching her.

'Mistress?'

'It's nothing, Neave. And don't call me mistress, especially now.'

'I'm sorry.'

'Don't worry, nobody is around to notice.'

There was a voice from above them. 'Nobody is around to fecking notice what?'

'You might want to consider taking a look around before saying something like that.'

Maena looked up and saw the pest, Pockle. 'Oh, it's you.'

'And a cheery fecking hello to you too.'

Neave picked up a log from the pile of firewood next to the door. 'Don't worry, I've got it.'

As much as it pained her, it would probably be better if Neave didn't brain the annoying fairy. 'Put the log down, Neave.'

Neave hesitated, then dropped the log to the ground. It landed with a thump.

It was at this point that Snorri and Brynhild made an appearance from around the corner of the hut.

'More visitors. I'm not sure you lot understand what it means to be a hermit,' said Snorri.

'Hello, Brynhild,' said Maena.

Brynhild broke into a broad grin. 'Hevac, old son!' In one hand she held a brace of dead rabbits and she extended the other towards Hevac.

Maena looked at Brynhild's outstretched hand warily.

'She expects an arm-clasp.'

Of course. Maena clasped forearms with Brynhild who, putting down the rabbits, thumped her on the back with her other hand.

'Good to see you,' said Brynhild.

'Uh, likewise,' said Maena.

Brynhild released her arm and stepped back, regarding her with a puzzled expression. 'I didn't think you were leaving the farm.'

'Events have precipitated myself and Neave leaving Saltrock.'

'Sounds juicy. You'll have to give me the details.'

'We have already spoken to Bienia. She has agreed to help us.'

'No fecking surprises there.' Pockle winked suggestively at Maena.

'*That fairy is so...uncouth.*'

Well, at least that's something I can agree with Hevac on, thought Maena.

'Any friend of Bienia and Brynhild's is a friend of mine. Come in, have some tea. I'll cook some tasty rabbit stew,' said Snorri.

'That would be acceptable,' said Maena.

'Got anything fecking stronger?' asked Pockle.

Bienia hadn't had much time to digest what Hevac had told her before the hut was suddenly full of dwarves and a fairy. Snorri made sure all his guests had a beverage of their choice. This was tea for the dwarves, and a thimble full of parsnip vodka for Pockle. Bienia drank her tea and quietly watched Hevac. There was something odd about his behaviour. Odder than usual, that is. She wondered what had happened on the island to force him to leave the farm.

'So, tell me, what brings you here?' asked Brynhild.

'As I have discussed with Bienia, King Oberon has returned and we need help to defeat him,' said Hevac.

Pockle coughed, spraying vodka in a thin cloud in front of him. 'Feck,' he said.

'Pockle? What's the matter?' asked Bienia.

Pockle held up a forefinger, drained the remaining vodka from the thimble then wiped his mouth with the back of his hand. 'The King Oberon?'

'Yes,' said Hevac.

Pockle held out the thimble towards Snorri. 'More fecking booze.'

Snorri poured a measure of the spirit into the thimble. The fairy drank it in a single gulp and held the thimble out for a refill. Snorri silently refilled it.

'Pockle, is he that bad?' asked Brynhild.

'You better sodding believe it.'

'The vermin is correct, he is that bad,' said Hevac.

'Less of the vermin, goat-boy,' said Pockle.

'Both of you, stop,' said Bienia. The last thing she needed was for Hevac and Pockle to start an argument.

Hevac lowered his head. 'Sorry, Bienia.'

'Whatever,' said Pockle.

She supposed that was as close as she was going to get to an apology from the fairy.

'What's so bad?' asked Brynhild.

Pockle peered up at her, swaying gently. 'He can glamour you just like that.' He snapped his fingers.

'Like the svalfae?' asked Bienia.

'Worse. He doesn't have to muck about with daggers and blood. Just has to sodding look at you and you're done.'

Hevac was nodding. 'It is horrible.'

Brynhild scratched her head. 'Sounds dangerous. Why can't you just stay here? Surely the goat farm isn't worth it.'

'Fecking right it isn't,' muttered Pockle.

Hevac shook his head sadly. 'Alas, it is not that simple. Oberon is planning to bring the world under his dominion.'

'What, all of it?' asked Bienia.

'Yes. All of it. He is preparing the invasion as we speak,' said Hevac.

Snorri coughed. 'Sounds to me, that we need some heavy duty magical assistance.'

'Got any ideas, uncle?' asked Brynhild.

'We should go and see the mystics of the Spiky mountains.'

'And they can help?' asked Bienia.

'Either that or they will know who can,' said Snorri.

'Then we should go and see these mystics,' said Hevac.

Bienia sighed. 'So much for going home for the holidays. Why can't everything just stay saved?'

CHAPTER 12

John's back had transitioned from being agonisingly painful to merely hurting like hell. The day after his punishment, the ship's surgeon had paid them a visit and smeared a grey paste into the raw wounds on their backs. To say this had 'stung a little' would be an understatement. John hoped that the fact it hurt so much proved that it was doing him some good although he still entertained the sneaking suspicion that it was a part of their punishment. Jimmy had passed out during the application of the paste and had so far not woken up.

'Jimmy.' He leant over and gently shook the other man's shoulder being careful not to touch his back. 'Jimmy.'

Jimmy's eyes flickered open. 'Mum?'

'It's John.'

'John?' Jimmy turned his head to look at him.

'You okay?' asked John.

'Oh no.' Jimmy's face went from confused to despair. 'I was having a lovely dream.'

'Sorry.'

'It's not your fault.' Jimmy frowned. 'Wait a minute, it is your fault.'

'Sorry,' repeated John. His regret at attacking the reaver was now being joined by regret for waking Jimmy up.

'You stupid bastard. What did you expect to happen?'

'I said I'm sorry,' said John.

'Just don't do anything else stupid.' With a pained groan, Jimmy slowly sat up.

John decided to stop apologising, it didn't seem to be doing him any good.

'We need to sit tight and hope we are sold. Things will get a bit better then,' said Jimmy.

'Better?'

'Better as in: not doomed to a life on the oar. Hopefully we'll get sold to a farmer or something.'

'Oh.'

'Yeah. I heard they have massive plantations down south, all worked by slaves. They get to have families too.'

'A family?'

'Yeah. They get new slaves that way. I didn't figure on settling down just yet, but a farmer is what we should hope for. Or a house slave. That can be a cushy number.'

'Sounds awful,' said John.

'Beats some of the alternatives,' said Jimmy.

'Does it?'

'Yeah, like the oars.' He nodded upwards. 'Or the fighting pits.'

'Gods,' said John.

Julienne had only been able to watch the first couple of lashes before she had to look away. This only gave her partial relief as she could still hear the crack of the whip and John and then Jimmy's cries of pain. After the punishment was over, she managed to persuade the captain to send the ships surgeon to treat the two men's backs. It was fortunate that the captain had taken a liking to her so she could even make such a suggestion. However, she knew this would only last until they reached Olong where she would be sold for a great deal of money. That is, she would be if she didn't escape. This was something Julienne fully intended to do, and to do that she needed the captain to be off guard when they finally reached Olong.

'You are lost in thought my pretty flower. Tell me, what it is that you are thinking about?' The captain was lying on a sleeping pallet, hands behind his head. The sheets were pulled down, exposing a hairy, well-tanned chest. He was speaking in Aravic, the tongue of the ancient Arann empire. The empire itself was long gone, but it had left a linguistic legacy on the lands to the south of the Pockveld. Julienne was, of course, fluent.

She stopped looking out at the waves through the small porthole in the cabin wall and turned her head to look at him. 'Nothing of consequence,' she said in accented Aravic.

'Then you should come and please your master.' He patted the space next to him.

Julienne smiled and walked over to the bed. 'You are not tired then?'

'I do not think I could ever tire of your beauty, my sweet northern flower.'

She inwardly grimaced at the cloying sweetness of his words. Outwardly, her smile turned sultry. 'Oh, we will have to see about that.'

Over the last few days and nights, she had arranged for the captain of the Illian reavers to become infatuated with her. It had not been difficult. When he had summoned her to his cabin, she feigned enthusiasm and encouraged his image of himself as a great lover.

'We should at least try,' agreed the captain.

Julienne knelt next to him on the sleeping pallet, put her hand on his thigh, leaned down into an energetic kiss, and began the attempt.

CHAPTER 13

The captain's dead eyes stared vacantly at the ceiling of the grubby inn room. Julienne wiped the blade of his knife clean on his shirt and then knelt and tucked it into her boot. She studied the man's expression, still locked in surprise at being stabbed, then drew her hand over his face, closing his eyes.

She jerked her head up, startled at a sudden shout from outside the window, then relaxed as she realised it was just a street-trader hawking his wares. Julienne quickly searched the body, liberating a small leather pouch of coins, then moved to the door and cracked it open. The landing was clear, so she slipped out and gently closed the door behind her.

Once she was outside the inn, she ducked into an alleyway and took stock of her possessions, quickly counting the coins she had found on the captain. Nineteen sheks and a handful of ki, the smaller denomination coins. So she had enough money to last awhile and even use for bribes if she had to. Apart from her newfound wealth, she also had a knife tucked in her boot. So far so good. However, without John, she did not have a way of infiltrating the warlord's army. She now had conflicting priorities: to continue with the mission plan and try to make contact with any local assets that remained or locate John and free him from captivity. With the Banshee gone, she knew that the first task was more important to the mission as she would need help to get intelligence back to Asterland. On the other hand, the mission be damned. She was going to find out what had happened to her boyfriend.

With the coin pouch safely tucked into a pocket, she stepped back out onto the street. If she remembered correctly the slave market was nearby. She approached the street-trader she had heard earlier. He was selling dried fruit from a small handcart.

'Excuse me gentle-sir, could you tell me the way to the slave market?' Her Aravic was accented. This, along with her clothes which were those of an Astish servant, marked her out as a foreigner.

The street-trader squinted at her. 'Buy a tasty pear, lady, and I will direct you to the warlord's palace itself.'

Julienne put her hand in her pocket and pulled a couple of coins out of the pouch. 'Two ki?'

'Four.'

Julienne tutted, but handed over the coins. She didn't have time to haggle.

The street-trader handed her a dried pear, then pointed down the street. 'That way.'

'Thankyou,' said Julienne.

When she arrived at the slave market, the morning's auction was already underway. Julienne sighed with relief when she saw John and Jimmy with the slaves waiting to be auctioned.

She stayed at the back of the crowd and kept a low profile until the auction of her friends. The auctioneer started, as he had with all the other slaves sold that morning, by extolling the virtues of this pair of northern slaves. Apparently they were hard workers and fine physical specimens. A low murmur and a collective sucking of air between teeth came from the crowd when their shirts were removed so potential buyers could assess their physique. The wounds on their backs were still fresh, marking the pair as troublemakers who had required punishment.

The bidding was slow and stopped at seventeen sheks. Julienne felt the weight of the coins in her pocket. She had to try, this was an opportunity to buy them and secure their freedom. She knew a woman buying slaves was rare, but not unheard of. Hopefully, she wouldn't draw too much attention to herself.

'Eighteen sheks.' Her voice cut across the noise of the crowd and several people turned to look at this new female bidder. Her hood was up and her face was concealed in shadow.

'Twenty sheks.' The original bidder sounded angry.

'Any advance on twenty?' asked the auctioneer.

Julienne cursed and remained silent. She didn't have enough money to outbid him.

The auctioneer waited a few more seconds, waiting for another bid, before pointing at the winning bidder. 'Fine. Sold for twenty sheks to Unteen.'

At least she now had a name to put to the sour face of John and Jimmy's new master. Unteen.

CHAPTER 14

Squat white-washed buildings crouched under the slowly rising heat of the morning sun. The Olong slave market was in a large square, partially filled by cages which held the human merchandise to be sold that day. Next to this was the auction block – a raised wooden platform on which the unfortunate souls being sold were displayed.

The auctioneer was a fat man, dressed in a grubby, off-white shirt and baggy trousers. 'Who will give me thirty sheks for this fine pair of northerners?'

Murmurs spun around the crowd, but no bids were forthcoming.'

'Twenty five? They've got to be worth that at least.' The auctioneer was sweating profusely, the damp patches under his arms testament to the heat of the midday sun.

'I'll give you fifteen.' The speaker had a jagged white scar down the right side of his face. It crossed a milky white eye and ran down his cheek to his dark beard.

'Fifteen! Any advance on fifteen? These two can give you years of useful labour.'

John hadn't understood a word of the auction so far. He looked around the faces of the crowd. They were looking at him and Jimmy appraisingly, like cattle at the markets back home in Asterland. The state of their backs probably marked them out as potential troublemakers; they did not seem to be fetching a good price.

The auctioneer was despairing of getting a good price for the foreigners when there was another bid, a voice clear and high from the back of the crowd. 'Eighteen sheks.'

The auctioneer frowned slightly. The bidder was a woman and, by her accent, foreign. Still, her coin would be as good as anyone's and her bid would help push up the price.

'Twenty,' responded the first bidder. He scanned the rear of the crowd, his eyes flashing with smouldering anger.

'Any advance on twenty?'

There was no response from the mystery bidder.

The auctioneer sighed almost inaudibly. That would have to do. 'Fine. Sold for twenty sheks to Unteen.'

John and Jimmy were manhandled off the auction block and taken back and put in a smaller cage. One of the slave-wranglers marked a slate with chalk and hung it on a hook fixed to the door of the cage.

'I think we've just been sold,' said John.

Jimmy looked up at him. 'Yeah. Did he look like a farmer to you?'

'Not really,' said John.

'Maybe he was. Farmers carry swords in Olong right?'

John shook his head. 'Do they? He looked like a bandit, right out of the stories, to me.'

'Shit,' said Jimmy. 'Do bandits buy slaves?'

'All I know about Olong is what Julienne told me about it when we were on the Banshee.'

'And?' asked Jimmy.

John shrugged. 'She overlooked giving me a run down on the slave economy.'

By the end of the auction, John had gained first hand knowledge of the workings of Olong's slave economy. Three other men had joined them in the cage over the course of the morning. These three dark-skinned men kept to themselves, speaking to themselves in a lilting language that John had not heard before. Once the sale had finished, their new owner collected his merchandise, and the five of them were loaded onto a horse-drawn wagon and taken along Olong's dusty streets.

Soon, they left the city proper and joined a road heading east, away from the coast, eventually reaching a vast sprawling camp. A sea of tents stretched out across the hillside, brightly coloured pennants fluttering above some of the more gaudily decorated. John, Jimmy and the other new purchases were unloaded and taken to a large, drab, and less important looking tent. There, they were made to stand in a line, almost as if they were soldiers on parade. A man dressed in a chainmail shirt with a scimitar at his waist approached. He was accompanied by two women. One had hair and skin as black as midnight and wore a swirling dress of deep green. The other was older, her leathery skin tanned a deep brown. She peered out at them from under a mop of scruffy grey hair. The man barked something in Aravic, the language spoken in Olong, and nodded at the two women. The first approached the three dark-skinned men and started to speak to them in their strange lilting language.

The older woman walked up to John and Jimmy.

'My name is Dora. You are now members of the host of warlord Karvarl. You will be trained to fight by spear-captain Jak,' she indicated the man in the chainmail shirt, 'and in the Aravic language by me. Nod if you understand.'

Both John and Jimmy nodded.

'This is the spear of Jak's tent. When not training you will stay here. Now, you will be marked.'

The old woman looked at them appraisingly. 'You know when to stay quiet. Good.'

John heard a short scream of pain. A swarthy man with an eyepatch and a grin punctuated by missing teeth was pressing a red hot iron rod into the shoulder of one of the other slaves.

'Gods,' said John.

'They won't help you here,' said Dora.

The hot iron came away to reveal a burn in the shape of a spear with a letter of the Aravic script on either side.

'What is it?' asked Jimmy.

'That is what marks you as a member of Jak's spear,' said Dora.

John watched apprehensively as one by one the others were branded. Then, it was his left arm being held out. He instinctively tried to pull it back, but the man's hand was like a vice around his wrist. He let out an involuntary cry as the hot iron sank into his shoulder, filling his nostrils with the smell of cooking flesh.

The man released his wrist and the initial searing pain faded to a burning throb. He put his right hand to the burn and pulled it away as the brush of his fingertips produced fresh needles of agony.

'Now you go in there.' Dora pointed to the tent.

John looked at her dumbly for a moment before following the others inside. Inside were rows of crude camp beds. Most had someone either lying or sitting on them. There was a low hubbub of conversation, all of it in Aravic. It quieted when they entered, and a large man with dark hair and a dark beard rose from his seated position on the bed near the tent flap. He said something in Aravic and pointed to the back of the tent where there were half a dozen empty beds.

John noticed the man had the same brand they had just received on his left shoulder. So this man was a slave as well. Anyway, he got the gist of what they were being told to do and followed Jimmy to the back of the tent.

Jimmy sat down on the camp bed. 'On the bright side, it's not the fighting pits and I've got something to take my mind off the pain of my back.'

John laughed shortly. 'I suppose so.'

The man on the bed next to John's looked at them with surprise. 'You... you're Astish.'

'Yes,' said John.

The man's face broke into a smile. 'It's good to hear an Astish voice. My name's Eric.' He extended a hand in greeting.

'John, and this is Jimmy.' John took the man's hand and Eric shook it enthusiastically.

Eric started to talk in a fast excited babble. 'Where are you from? I'm from Yevon; not recently, of course; my family still live there; I was posted in Fort May.'

'Fort May? Isn't that where——'

'The nomads attacked? Yes. They took some of us as slaves and brought us to Olong to sell.'

'And you ended up in the warlord's army? Funny old world,' said Jimmy.

'What about you two?'

'Our ship was taken by Illian reavers. They came to Olong and...' John spread is hands expansively.

'So, recent?' asked Eric.

'Last week,' said Jimmy.

Eric leant forward. 'Any news? Did the nomads carry on? Did they reach Yevon?'

'Last we heard, they were still sitting in the fort,' said John.

'Thank the gods.' Eric leant back and ran his hand through his hair.

John was about to share his briefing on warlord Karvarl and the feared invasion of Asterland, but stopped himself. What did he actually know about this man? He could picture Julienne slowly shaking her head when she found out he had shared all his knowledge with a stranger.

'What's being in the warlord's army like?' asked Jimmy.

'Like?' Eric considered for a moment. 'Much like the Astish one. Except you don't get paid and there's no leave.'

The loud voice of spear-sergeant Jak interrupted any further discussion on the working conditions of a slave soldier.

'What's he saying?' asked John.

'Time for fighting practice,' said Eric.

'They give us weapons?' asked Jimmy.

'Of course.' Eric reached under his camp bed and grabbed a long wooden pole from underneath it. Once he had pulled it out, John realised it was a spear. The other men in the tent were doing the same.

'I don't have one of those,' said Jimmy. He had bent over and was looking under his bed.

'You'll get one soon enough.' Eric beckoned for them to follow. 'Come on, you don't want to be late.'

With no other choice, John and Jimmy left the tent to begin their first day as slave soldiers in warlord Karvarl's host.

Reluctantly, Julienne turned her attention to making contact with the Astish spy network in Olong and finding how much of it was left since Macky's disappearance. She spent a day leaving messages at several of the dead drops used by Macky and his contacts; she had been given a list of those that Luke knew about. Julienne hoped that someone was still checking them and would get the message to meet her in one of the prearranged emergency meeting places: a tavern near the slave market.

It was on the fourth day of sitting at the designated table in the gloom towards the back of the tavern that Julienne's waiting paid off. A slight woman with a grimy scarf wrapped around her head and face sat next to her at the table and carefully placed a bottle of wine from the Sunset Isles and two cups on the table. She precisely poured a measure into each cup then held one of the drinking vessels towards Julienne and said, in fluent Aravic, 'The birds flew south early this year.'

Julienne took the cup and gave the return phrase, 'They must be confused by the spring storms.'

The other woman visibly relaxed. 'Thank the gods, I thought I was the only one left. The name's Magsi.'

'You can call me Adele.' A new city, a new alias.

The two women conversed quietly, their voices lost in the hubbub of conversation.

'You're the only one left in Olong?' asked Julienne.

'As far as I know.'

'Damn.'

'I was considering cutting my losses and heading for the border.'

'I may need you to do that. Head to the border I mean.'

The woman tilted her head slightly. 'How so?'

'Someone needs to report on what's happening here.'

The woman made no comment, but raised an eyebrow in query.

'When I've found out what that is, obviously.'

'Obviously,' said Magsi.

'Do you have anything to report?' asked Julienne.

'Apart from the alarming disappearance of the entire spy network here in Olong?'

'Yes, apart from that.'

'Well, there's a massive recruitment drive on for warlord Karvarl's host.'

'Go on.'

'All the mercenaries in the city states seem to be here and the warlord's slave buyer is buying every male slave that can hold a spear. The army encampment is going to be larger than the city if they keep this up.'

'Does this slave buyer have a name?' asked Julienne.

Magsi smiled. 'Of course. Unteen.'

Now, at least, Julienne knew where John was,

'How would I go about infiltrating this army camp?'

'As a prostitute?'

Julienne sighed. 'Of course.'

Magsi shrugged. 'You did ask.'

'Maybe there's another way.' Julienne nodded at two men who were having a loud conversation at the bar.

The men wore sword belts and had the air of military men. Loud and crude.

'Officers from the camp,' said Magsi.

One of the men was complaining loudly to his companion about the gods-forsaken Astish slaves in his spear and the shortage of language instructors in the camp. Apparently, speaking both Aravic, the language of the old empire, and Elend, the language of the north, was a rare talent.

'I have an idea. I'll see you later, Magsi,' said Julienne.

'I'll visit the drop every day.' Magsi stood, leaving her cup and bottle on the table, and made her way out of the tavern.

Julienne waited a minute before she picked up her cup of wine and walked over to the bar.

'Excuse me, gentle-sir. I couldn't help overhearing,' she said in Aravic before switching to Elend, her native tongue. 'Perhaps I could be of assistance?'

The two men stopped talking and turned to face her.

'An Asterlander?'

She gave a slight bow.

'You seek employment?'

'Yes, gentle-sir.'

'Your name?'

'Adele, gentle-sir.'

The man nodded curtly. 'Then you start now. You will return with me to camp.'

Julienne nodded again. 'Yes, gentle-sir.'

'You will refer to me as spear-sergeant Valun.'

'Yes, spear-sergeant Valun.'

Valun drained his cup and wiped his mouth with the back of his hand. 'Welcome to warlord Karvarl's host, tutor Adele.'

CHAPTER 15

The snow-capped peaks of the Spiky mountains were visible on the horizon. The sky was a brilliant blue, the only clouds faint and wispy high in the sky. The road, what there was of it, wended its way into the undulating foothills. Bienia took a bite out of her trail-biscuit, gazed out at the view from the crest of the hill and listened to the others talk while she munched her way through the dry oaty food.

'Do you believe the stories?' asked Brynhild.

'Stories?' asked Hevac.

'About the Trollkin clan who live in the mountains.'

Snorri took a deep pull on his pipe, exhaled a billowing cloud of smoke, and looked thoughtful. 'When I last passed that way, I saw no sign of dwarf inhabitants. Sign of trolls, for sure, but no dwarves.'

'Good,' said Brynhild. 'Not that there were signs of trolls, but that the trollkin are just a story.'

'Probably,' said Snorri.

'Probably?' Brynhild put her hand on her sword hilt. 'Gods. If they exist and even half the stories are true.' She shivered.

'There's usually at least a little truth in old tales,' said Snorri.

'I would like to hear these stories,' said Hevac.

'I would rather not,' said Brynhild.

'Would it not be better to be prepared?' asked Hevac.

Bienia finished up her trail-biscuit and went to join the others at the side of the rough hill trail they were following. 'Once Pockle returns from his scouting flight, we should get going. I'd like to make a few more miles before nightfall.'

Brynhild stood up and then helped Snorri to his feet.

Snorri dusted himself down and massaged his thighs. 'Thankyou, Brynhild. I haven't done this much walking for quite some time.'

'Maybe you should have stayed at home,' said Bienia.

Snorri shook his head and laughed. 'Ah, I'm not so decrepit that I can't embark on a quest, lass.'

'A quest? I don't think so.' Bienia didn't really consider what she was doing as a quest. More like just doing what had to be done. Hopefully for money.

Snorri put his hand on her shoulder. 'Don't sound so doubtful, lass. We have a group of heroes, just like in the sagas, and we're going to stop the King of the fey-folk from taking over. Sounds an awful lot like a quest to me.'

'When you put it like that, I suppose it does,' said Bienia.

'Put what like fecking what?' Pockle was spiralling down, returning from his high aerial reconnaissance.

'Uncle Snorri was just telling us how we were all heroes,' said Brynhild.

Pockle landed on Brynhild's shoulder. 'Well, you obviously are.'

'Thankyou, Pockle. And a point made without swearing, well done,' said Brynhild.

'Feck.'

'Anything to report?' asked Bienia.

'There's a couple of troll-holes south of the trail about half a mile on, but I couldn't see any bugger moving around,' said Pockle.

'Hopefully we'll be well past them by the time they come out for their night time hunting,' said Bienia.

'We won't be if we hang around here gabbing,' said Snorri.

'The old one is right,' said Hevac.

Bienia was worried about Hevac. He had been behaving oddly since their reunion. She had initially put it down to the trauma of leaving his goats behind, but when she had broached the subject of the farm he had been dismissive. She resolved to speak with Neave about him in private later.

Maena would be glad to be out of this vessel. There were a number of things wrong with it. At the moment the most bothersome was its reaction to being around Bienia. If she let her mind wander, she found it journeying to daydreams of intimacy with the shieldmaiden which, although pleasant, were obviously brought on by inhabiting this particular vessel. Having the original owner hanging around in the back of her mind probably had something to do with it.

Getting a new vessel was something that would take time and the proper blood magic. Finding a vessel and performing the rituals would have to wait for now. She looked sidelong at Neave, walking beside her. Now there was a willing vessel.

'*Don't even think about it.*' Hevac's voice rang loudly in her head.

Maena sighed and looked down at her feet as she walked along the trail. Very well, she would find someone else if possible.

'*No. Definite. I will not lose my sister.*'

Maena looked up at the horizon and mentally changed the subject: At least the mountains were looking a little closer.

'*Don't think I will make it easy for you to take Neave. I will do everything in my power to frustrate you.*'

The trouble was, Hevac could quite easily disrupt the ritual by interrupting her concentration. She needed his cooperation.

'*And you will have it. But not for Neave.*'

'Are you alright, Hevac?' asked Bienia.

'Hmm?' Maena continued putting one foot in front of the other.

'That was a big sigh, and you're being awfully quiet.'

'Just thinking.'

Bienia moved a little closer and put a hand on the goatherd's arm. Maena felt a thrill of excitement.

'Please, you can tell me if something is bothering you,' said Bienia.

No I can't, thought Maena.

'*You shouldn't keep lying to her.*'

'I will. Do not worry about me.' Lying is exactly what she would keep doing.

'What about Neave? She has said hardly anything since we left Snorri's hut.' Bienia glanced back over her shoulder at Hevac's sister.

'Do not worry about her either.' Maena lifted Bienia's hand from her arm.

'Well, I'm sorry for being concerned.'

Maena did not think Bienia sounded sorry. Great, now she had upset the shieldmaiden. Why did that make her feel awful?

'I'm sorry, Bienia. There are some things I cannot tell you about now. I will when the time is right.'

'*Will you?*'

Maena was moderately surprised to realise she had meant it. When the time was right, she would tell Bienia the truth.

The campfire had burnt low when Bienia got her chance. She was on watch, sitting by the fire, her cloak pulled around her against the cold, when she saw Neave get up and head for the nearby bushes. She waited for the sound of splashing to stop before following.

'Neave?'

'What? Who is it?'

Bienia saw Neave emerge from behind a bush doing up her belt.

'It's Bienia. Can we talk?'

'Talk? Sorry. Yes of course.' Neave looked a little bewildered.

'About Hevac.'

Bienia knew something was wrong the instant she said Hevac's name. Neave looked like a dwarf caught with her hand in the ale cupboard.

'What about him?'

'He is not himself.'

'Isn't he?'

'You said so yourself.'

'I did? I suppose so. I can't think what I meant. Time for bed, goodnight.'

Bienia grabbed her arm as Neave tried to go around her. 'There is something wrong. What is it?'

She had a terrible feeling she recognised the character traits Hevac was showing. She had, after all, lived with them for over a year. Maena. Could it be true? She thought back to the kiss at the hut. Hevac had definitely kissed her back.

'Wrong? I—'

Bienia squeezed Neave's arm. 'Don't lie to me, Neave. Is it Maena?'

'You're hurting me.' Neave tried to pull away but Bienia's grip was too strong.

'Tell me.' Bienia's voice was loaded with quiet menace.

Neave's eyes moistened, and a tear rolled down her left cheek. 'Yes. It is my mistress. I didn't expect her to—Hevac will be alright.'

'Damn it Neave. What else is a lie? King Oberon? The invasion?'

'That is all true. I swear it,' said Neave.

'I thought Maena was going to be his queen?'

'The King was, ah, not in agreement,' said Neave.

'I see,' said Bienia. 'And the invasion?'

'That is as my mistress told you.'

If that was true, and she didn't think Neave was lying, then helping Maena destroy King Oberon was in everyone's interest. Bienia let go of Neave and rubbed her face with her hands. Bryn and Pockle weren't going to like it, and the gods alone knew what would Maena do when once her secret was out.

'Are you going to tell the others?' asked Neave.

'No. And in return, you will not tell Maena about this conversation.'

Neave nodded hesitantly. 'And you will still help?'

'We still need to stop the King. So, for now, yes.'

CHAPTER 16

The sky was sullen and grey, hanging low over the craggy peaks. The dwarves had spent the morning following a trail that threaded its lonely way up the side of one of the mountains. Bienia shivered. The air was noticeably colder up here.

'Is it much further?' Neave panted out her question from behind Bienia.

Bienia looked over her shoulder. The young dwarf was struggling somewhat. She was not used to this much walking, especially uphill. In contrast, Hevac seemed to be taking it all in his stride. She still thought of him as Hevac even though she now knew that Maena was in the coachman's seat.

In front of Bienia were Brynhild and Snorri, who was leading the way.

'Nearly there,' said Snorri.

'And where, exactly, is there?' asked Brynhild.

'A cave,' said Snorri.

'We could have stayed in the Troll-fells and gone to a cave,' said Brynhild.

'Not one with Mystics in it,' said Snorri.

'Oh. I thought they lived in the valleys,' said Brynhild.

'Most do, but not these two. They're near the summit of this mountain.' said Snorri.

'For the Gods' sake, why?' asked Brynhild.

'They can launch their balloon higher,' said Snorri.

Bienia thought she must have misheard. 'Excuse me?'

'Their balloon. Quicker to get in amongst it,' said Snorri.

'In amongst what?' asked Bienia.

'The storm. You know, thunder and lightning.'

There was a flash, followed moments later by a loud crack and rumble of thunder, as if to punctuate Snorri's revelation.

Pockle poked his head out of Brynhild's backpack. 'What's all the bleeding noise?' He looked up at the clouds as the rain started. 'Oh, that's just bloody great.'

They all stopped to don their rain-cloaks. Bienia's hair was already soaked by the time she pulled up the green hood of her cloak. 'I hope you're right about it being close.'

'Come on, we should hurry,' said Snorri.

By the time they reached their destination, the rest of Bienia had joined her hair being soaked. She thought that Snorri needed to work on his definition of 'almost there'. The mouth of the cave had been blocked off with a wooden wall. Large dollops of pitch had been slathered over it, providing water-proofing. On the left of the wall, light was bleeding out around the edges of a door.

The sound of Snorri banging his fist on the door was carried away by the wind. He continued to hammer away until the door opened slightly offering a tantalisingly narrow strip of light and warmth to the bedraggled travellers.

A thin-faced youth peered around the door. 'Yes?'

'Is that you, Wynn?'

'Yes. Wait... Hang on, is that old Snorri?'

'Yes, and less of the old.'

Wynn's face broke into a wide smile and he fully opened the door. 'Come in! You must be soaked.' He noticed the others. 'And your friends.'

'Thankyou, Wynn.'

Wynn stepped to one side, allowing them all to troop inside before shutting the weather outside. 'Da will be pleased to see you.'

'I see you've fixed up the door,' said Snorri.

'Yes, yes. You were right, of course, it is much warmer with all the gaps filled.'

A voice shouted from further inside the cave. 'Wynn, who are you talking to lad?'

'It's Snorri, Da,' answered Wynn.

'Snorri? Bring him through, bring him through!'

'Hang your cloaks and come on through.' Wynn pointed to a row of rusty iron hooks set into the rock by the entrance.

Once the party had divested themselves of their wet weather gear, they followed Wynn deeper into the cave. Inside there were a number of flickering lanterns that lit the interior with an unsteady yellow light. There was a lot of clutter which scattered shadows over the rough-hewn rock walls. The air smelled of wood-smoke from an open fire over which a battered black kettle was hanging. A thin stream of steam escaped upward with the smoke into a narrow hole in the roof of the cave.

Sitting in a wooden chair, beside a crackling fire, was a man with wild grey hair and an untidy beard. 'Snorri, you pick a stormy night to come visiting.'

'Hello, Dylan,' said Snorri.

'And you have brought companions. What brings you back to the mountains?'

'We seek knowledge of the King of the fey-folk,' said Snorri.

'Specifically, how to kill the bastard,' said Pockle.

Dylan stood up and pointed at Pockle who had just stuck his head out of Brynhild's pack to deliver the clarification. 'A fairy! Gods, hide the shoes Wynn, I'll get the net.'

'Calm down. It's me, Pockle, you daft bugger.'

'Oh!' Dylan sat back down again. 'That is a relief. You did give me a start.'

'You know Pockle?' asked Brynhild.

'I'm afraid so,' said Dylan. 'Wynn, get some extra seats for our guests.'

'Yes, Da.' Wynn scuttled away into the back of the cave.

'Now, tea.' Dylan picked up a grubby looking cloth, wrapped it around his hand and then lifted the lid from the kettle. He took a deep sniff and, appearing satisfied, replaced the lid.

By the time he was pouring the first cup of murky grey liquid from the kettle into a wooden cup, Wynn had returned with a stack of small wooden stools.

Soon, everyone was seated around the fire holding a cup of hot murky grey liquid. Bienia sniffed hers—it smelled earthy. She eyed it suspiciously. 'Is it safe?'

'Define safe,' said Snorri.

Dylan frowned. 'Please, Snorri. You have had the special mystic tea before. You know it will not kill you.'

Snorri nodded. 'Aye, that is true. It won't kill you.'

'Will it do anything else?' asked Bienia.

'It will reveal to you the mysteries of the universe,' said Dylan.

Brynhild was now also looking at her tea suspiciously.

'Hang on a minute, is this that mushroom tea you told me about, Uncle Snorri?'

'Yes,' said Snorri.

'Uh. Do we have to drink it?' asked Bienia. Bryn had told her that she suspected that it was the mystic's mushroom tea that had made Snorri 'go a bit strange'.

'It is an essential part of the hospitality of the mystics,' said Dylan.

'You couldn't just give us a biscuit, or something?' asked Bienia.

'A biscuit? Gods, you don't want one of them,' said Snorri. 'Stick with the tea.'

Brynhild shrugged. 'Like you say, it won't kill us. Bottoms up.' She lifted her cup and swallowed a mouthful of the earthy liquid.

'You fecking sure that's a good idea?' asked Pockle. He had not been offered any tea and had declared he didn't want any anyway as 'it wasn't a proper fecking drink'.

'It tastes of feet,' said Brynhild.

Hevac made a show of sniffing his cup. 'It does.' He then drank some.

'Just marched twenty miles feet, or just had your monthly bath feet?' asked Bienia.

'Bath feet. Maybe a day after.' Brynhild took another sip. 'Make that two days.'

'Not so bad then,' said Bienia, and she followed Brynhild's lead. The tea tasted of old pipe smoke and was slightly lumpy in texture. She chewed one of the lumps contemplatively.

'Ah, what the hell. Here we go again.' Snorri swallowed a mouthful of his tea.

The others then went ahead and drank theirs.

Bienia swallowed the now thoroughly masticated lump. 'What now?'

'Now, we wait,' said Dylan.

'Oh. What can you tell us about this fairy King?' asked Bienia.

'Patience. We will speak afterwards,' said Dylan.

'After what?' asked Hevac.

Snorri chuckled. 'You'll see.'

'See what?' Bienia was getting a bit fed up with all this vagueness.

'Just listen to the rain and open your mind,' said Dylan.

Bienia sighed. It looked like they wouldn't get any information out of these weirdos until this 'hospitality of the mystics' had run its course. She gave up talking and listened to the weather outside. She was glad they were inside, next to the fire.

They remained in awkward silence, waiting for something to happen.

Bienia looked around the cave. It was quite homely and a bit messy. The walls were decorated with wild spiralling abstract designs painted in bold primary colours. Pots and pans were stacked in one corner, and next to them were several green bottles, dusty with age. She watched with interest as one of the bottles moved upwards slightly and then rejoined the others. The background noise of the rain and wind on the front door created a rhythmic beat and all the bottles started to ripple up and down in time to the beat.

'Bee, your face,' said Brynhild.

Bienia turned to look at her friend. She looked like she was wearing a deep purple eyeshadow. When had Bryn start wearing eyeshadow?

'The spiral. It's the spiral.' Snorri was off his stool and was standing next to the wall, tracing a red spiral with his hand.

Dylan stood behind the dwarf at the wall put his hands on Snorri's shoulders. 'The spiral is everything.'

'The stone is the power,' said Snorri. There was wonder in his voice.

'And the power is the stone,' said Hevac. 'Wait, what's going on?'

'Mistress,' said Neave, clutching Hevac's arm.

Bienia giggled. Neave just called Hevac mistress.

'You're all off your fecking tits,' said Pockle.

Brynhild stroked the fairy's face with her little finger. 'Don't be mean. You are so beautiful.'

Bienia realised something strange was going on, so she decided to investigate the interesting wood grain on an old chest that was near the bottles. Maybe they had been inspired by the pattern to start dancing. The grain runs true. The grain ran true. The grain. It is true.

CHAPTER 17

Bienia cracked open an eye. The cave was dimly lit by the embers off the fire. She was lying on the hard ground, her head on a duck down filled pillow. She opened her other eye and looked down at Hevac, his head resting on her leg. She had a peculiar empty feeling, like all her worries and troubles had been washed out of her. She stroked Hevac's hair and smiled.

'Mmph,' said Hevac.

'Morning,' said Bienia.

Hevac's eyes fluttered open, and he looked up into her eyes. 'Bienia. I...' He fell silent.

'Shh.' Bienia stroked his forehead. If he didn't talk, she could forget that Maena was in there with him.

'About time you fecking woke up.' Pockle was sitting cross-legged on one of the stools.

'Morning, Pockle.' Bienia was genuinely happy to see the fairy. She felt at peace with the world.

Brynhild sat up, her hair in disarray. 'Is it morning?'

Bienia heard the front door of the cave open and close, then Dylan and Snorri entered. Dylan was carrying an armful of firewood.

'Good, you are all awake,' said Dylan.

Hevac lifted Bienia's hand from his head and sat up. 'We need to talk about defeating King Oberon.'

Dylan nodded, dumped the logs next to the fire, picked up a stool from where it lay, forgotten on the floor, and sat down on it. 'King of the fey-folk.'

'That's him. An arrogant, ungrateful bastard,' said Hevac.

Bienia was momentarily surprised at the venom in Hevac's voice. She had never heard him talk like that before but, of course, it was Maena talking.

'Have you met him?' asked Dylan.

'Yes, both Neave and I have,' said Hevac in a terse, clipped voice.

'Where is Neave?' asked Bienia. She could see Snorri, Brynhild and Pockle, but Hevac's sister was missing.

'She is with Wynn, going to the stream for water,' said Dylan.

'Oberon. Tell me how to be rid of him,' said Hevac.

'If King Oberon is back, he is a threat to us all.'

'Yes, yes. A threat to us all. Now, do you know how to give him the final death?' asked Hevac.

'Tricky one,' said Dylan.

'Tricky one? The old dwarf told me that you would know,' said Hevac.

Snorri harrumphed. 'Now then. That's not what I said. I said that if anyone knew, it would be the mystics.'

'I said it was tricky, not that I couldn't help.'

'Out with it,' said Hevac. 'How do we kill him?'

'I also didn't say that I knew how to kill the King of the fey-folk.'

'Are you so annoying on purpose?' asked Hevac.

Bienia put a hand on his arm. Maena was not being

particularly diplomatic. 'Calm down. I'm sure he is getting to the point.' She looked significantly at Dylan. 'You are going to get to the point, right?'

'Yes, of course. The library of the mystics will have the answer you seek.'

Bienia sighed. 'Let me guess. It's many miles away guarded by some ferocious beast.'

Dylan smiled a knowing little smile. 'No. It is in Penworth.'

'And that is where exactly?' asked Hevac.

Bienia could feel the muscles in Hevac's arms tense. She momentarily forgot that Maena was in there and found herself thinking about how sexy she found Hevac's understated strength. She hurriedly let go of his arm and looked around at everyone, blushing slightly, worried that someone might realise what she was thinking about. Fortunately, everyone was focussed on Dylan, waiting for the mystic to bestow the knowledge of the library's location.

'In the valley, two miles east.'

Hevac let out a short laugh. 'That's it? No difficult quest? No map to find?'

'That's it,' said Dylan, mildly. 'You can go with Wynn this morning. He is going to pick up some supplies.'

'Thankyou, Dylan,' said Bienia.

'Oh, and I have a gift for you. It may help in your quest,' said Dylan.

'Our fecking what?' asked Pockle.

'Quest. It is what we mystics call it when a group of individuals embark on a great task to safeguard the world from danger.'

'I like the sound of that,' said Brynhild.

'Oh, there'll be tales sung about this,' said Snorri.

'The tale might be worth a few ales,' said Bienia.

'You mentioned a gift?' prompted Brynhild.

'Ah, yes.' Dylan retrieved a leather bag from a cupboard. There was a slight crackling noise emanating from inside the bag. He carefully passed it to Snorri.

'Is this what I think it is?' asked Snorri.

Dylan just smiled.

Snorri opened the bag and looked inside. His face was bathed in a flickering white light.

'What is it, uncle?' asked Brynhild.

'Lightning, lass. He's gone and given us a bottle of lightning.'

The dwarves gathered around the open bag and looked in awe at the bottle, its contents, fizzing and crackling, seemed barely contained.

'Given the importance of your undertaking, I thought it was the least I could do,' said Dylan. 'Please, do be careful with it, and only open the stopper if you really mean it.'

They arrived in Penworth in time for lunch. Wynn insisted that he would buy them food and took them to a stone built eating house called the 'Horny Snail'. The front wall was adorned by a large painting of a snail. Bienia wasn't sure it was anatomically accurate, but the artist had added a large organ to the snail which made it look like it was trying to pole vault over the front door.

Inside, everybody seemed to know Wynn and greeted him cheerfully. Lightning collecting seemed to be a prestigious occupation amongst the mystics. After he had reassured Janie, the round faced middle-aged lady who ran the establishment, that Pockle wasn't going to urinate anywhere he shouldn't, they settled down to eat. Lunch consisted of strips of cured mutton and bread.

'You don't expect me to bloody eat this do you?' Pockle was holding up a strip of the mutton.

'I'm sorry, little fella. Fresh meat is a luxury up here in the mountains,' said Wynn.

'Now I remember why I stayed clear of you lot when I lived up here. Well, apart from the occasional visit to piss in your shoes.'

Bienia almost spat her bread out laughing at the shocked look on Wynn's face.

'That was you? The mysterious shoe widdle incident?'

Pockle grinned. 'Fecking right. Always the left one.'

'Everyone wondered why it stopped so suddenly.'

'That's 'cos I left this fecking dump with the old duffer here.' Pockle pointed at Snorri.

Wynn nodded slowly. 'Well, all's well that ends well. It was good for Jason the cobbler's business. He was busy for months replacing everyone's wee soaked footwear.'

Bienia chewed and swallowed a mouthful of mutton. 'So, about this library.'

'I will take you there after lunch,' said Wynn.

There was a groan from Pockle. 'Fecking save me. The library?'

'You don't have to come. You can stay here with Brynhild. I'll go with Hevac and Snorri.'

'If it's all the same to you, lass, I'll stay here too,' said Snorri.

'That's probably for the best,' said Wynn.

'Why?' asked Bienia.

'Let's just say, I had my library privileges revoked last time I was here.' Snorri tapped the side of his nose.

'I'll have to get you to tell me about that visit sometime,' said Bienia.

'I was thinking of writing a memoir,' said Snorri.

'Then I'll make sure to read it.' Bienia smiled.

Brynhild belched. 'If we're staying here, do they serve beer?'

Wynn nodded. 'Yes. I'll ask Janie to bring you a jug.'

'Now you're fecking talking,' said Pockle.

The library was a two-storey stone building nestled in the centre of Penworth. It had plenty of high windows, all fitted with glass, presumably to let in light to read by.

Maena was glad to be away from the vermin's incessant swearing. She cast a sidelong glance at Bienia, admiring the way her short hair brushed the curve of her neck. She snapped her eyes away as she realised what she was doing. It was a good thing Neave was here to act as chaperone; she wasn't sure she could trust this vessel around the shieldmaiden. Its base urges were quite singular in their focus.

'I'll have you know that it is true love.'

True lust more like. Manea glanced at Bienia again. Yes, definitely lust.

They entered through a small wooden door into a large room filled with rows of bookcases. It smelt of dusty old books. A slight man with a pair of round wire-rimmed spectacles hanging around his neck on a piece of string was sorting through several stacks of books that completely covered a long oak desk. He looked up as the wind slammed the door shut behind them.

'Can I help you?'

'We're just here to browse,' said Bienia.

'Browse?' the man sounded offended.

'Yes. Browse. Is that a problem?' asked Maena.

'You are, of course, welcome to browse. However, I warn you that the cataloguing system is quite complex.'

'I'm sure we'll manage,' said Bienia.

'Very well.' The man sniffed and went back to his stack of books.

Maena led the way into the labyrinth of shelves.

'There are so many,' said Neave.

'We should split up,' said Bienia.

Maena nodded. 'Look for anything to do with fey-folk. Anything to do with King Oberon and blood magic rituals.'

Half an hour later, the three of them were back at the front desk.

The librarian was wearing a smug looking smile. 'Can I help you?'

'Yes,' said Bienia.

'Oh? Having trouble finding what you're looking for?'

Maena scowled. 'Of course we're having trouble. There's no rhyme or reason to how you've got things organised in here.'

'*There's no point getting angry with him. We need his help.*'

Maena refrained from continuing to berate the librarian. The goatherd was right, they needed help if they were to find anything useful in this chaotic mess of a library.

'I think you'll find the system is very efficient if you have sufficient knowledge and training to use it,' said the librarian.

'Yes, I'm sure it is,' said Bienia.

The librarian's smug smile widened. 'How may I assist you?'

'Books on fey-folk. Specifically, how to destroy King Oberon,' said Maena.

'Mmm. Interesting.' The librarian strode over to a large cabinet next to the book covered desk. It was six feet tall and had more drawers than Maena could comfortably count. He pulled out a drawer and started to flick slowly through hundreds of index cards.

'Can you hurry it up?' said Maena.

'*Considering you have lived for hundreds of years, you are quite impatient.*'

In her annoyance, Maena slipped and replied to Hevac out loud. 'And you can be quiet.'

'I assure you, I work better in silence,' said the librarian testily.

'Sorry about Hevac, he didn't mean offence.' Bienia shot her a strange look.

Maena inwardly cursed her sloppiness. It wasn't hard communicating internally, she needed to be more careful. 'Yes. I am sorry.'

'I accept your apology.' The librarian stopped leafing through the index cards. 'Here we are. Row C, shelf thirty-six. The Feyanomicum.'

'Feyanomicum? What sort of book title is that?' asked Bienia.

Maena's blood ran cold. That book. She had thought all the copies destroyed. 'Never heard of it.'

'*The book scares you?*'

Too damn right it scared her. That book contained the secrets and weaknesses of the fey-folk. All of the fey-folk, including her.

'I assure you, that is the book you want,' said the librarian.

Bienia shrugged. 'Okay, let's take a look.'

Armed with the location of the book, the three of them

re-entered the maze of shelving. Ten minutes later they had found the shelf. Now they had found it, Maena wondered how they had not seen it before. It was a large, leather-bound book, the title written down the spine in elaborate silver embossed letters. Bienia pulled it out from the shelf to reveal the cover, which was adorned with a silver spiral pattern that seemed to shift and move if you looked at it for more than a second.

Bienia took the book to one of the reading tables situated at the end of the rows of shelves and carefully opened it. 'Well, shit.'

'What is it?' asked Neave.

'It's not written in Elend or runes. I can't read it.'

'Let me,' said Maena.

'Fill your boots. What a waste of time,' said Bienia.

Maena could, of course, read the ancient language the book was written in. She flicked to the index in the back and scanned the list looking for King Oberon.

'Can you read it?' asked Bienia.

'Shh,' said Maena.

'What language is it?' asked Bienia.

Maena ignored the question as she leafed through the book until she found the correct page. Each page was written in a flowing cursive script interweaved with elaborate line drawings of the different fey-folk they described.

She'd never had the chance to read a copy of the Feyanomicum before. King Oberon had arranged for all copies of it destroyed centuries ago. She corrected herself: all but one copy of it.

As she read the page dedicated to King Oberon, her heart

sank. The blood ritual to destroy him was simple enough, it just required using a mage-forged blade.

'Just great.'

'What?' asked Bienia.

Maena continued reading.

'Maena, what is it? Talk to me.'

'*Oh, my. Bienia knows.*'

Maena looked up at Bienia's scowling face. 'What did you just say?'

'I asked you what you are reading,' said Bienia.

'You called me Maena.'

Bienia's eyes went wide. 'Damn it.'

'Did Neave tell you?'

'I am sorry my mistress,' said Neave.

'I think I already knew. She just confirmed it for me,' said Bienia.

'How long have you known?'

'A couple of days.'

'And you're still helping me?'

Bienia held her gaze. 'Yes. There is no way I'm leaving you in there with Hevac.'

'*I could kiss her.*'

So could I, thought Maena. Damn, she needed to get out of this vessel.

'It is not permanent. I will be more than happy to leave the goatherd when I have an opportunity.'

'What about Neave?' asked Bienia.

'*Not happening.*'

'For some reason, the goatherd objects to that idea.'

'But I would be honoured to be the vessel of my mistress,' said Neave.

'*No.*' Hevac's voice was strong. Definite.

'I'm afraid that Hevac's familial bond is too strong,' said Maena. 'Bienia. This can all wait until after King Oberon is dead.'

Bienia glared at her.

Maena pointed at the open book. 'Now, perhaps you will let me continue?'

Bienia simply nodded in response.

Maena returned to reading the book until she found what she was looking for. 'I hope you are ready for another journey.'

'Why?' asked Bienia.

'According to this book, it is possible to defeat the monarch of the fey-folk.'

'That's good isn't it?' asked Bienia.

'That is the good news. The bad news is that it involves a ritual using a specially forged dagger called "Defender of the righteous and the destroyer of the unclean".'

'That's a bit of a mouthful,' said Bienia.

'That's a direct translation from the ancient Aravic. It is called more simply "Feybane" in Elend.'

'Right. Why is that bad news?'

'It means we must retrieve this blade before we can deal with King Oberon.'

Bienia peered at the open pages as if she would suddenly understand the flowing script. 'Does it say where it is?'

'Yes.'

'Get to the point, Maena.'

'It is in the tomb of Emperor Yavin.'

'Who?'

'He led the Arann empire to victory in the war with the fey-folk. Feybane was buried with him.'

'There was a war with the fey-folk?'

Maena looked into the middle distance as she dredged up old memories best forgotten. 'A long time ago. Yavin forced King Oberon out of this realm, and now I know how he did it. Those damned battlemages of Kadrath forged Feybane.' Maena shivered. Those had been grim times. The humans had used blood magic against King Oberon. It had been totally unexpected and, after King Oberon was gone, the fey-folk who survived were scattered throughout the land. She and her sisters had started a new life on Saltrock.

'Then we best go and get it,' said Bienia.

Maena was conflicted. The blade was an anathema to her kind. She would be happy if the damned thing stayed buried forever. However, it looked like it was the only way to be rid of King Oberon.

'*The blade scares you?*'

'Does the book say where this fellow's tomb is?' asked Bienia.

Maena carefully tore the relevant page out of the book. 'It is near the city of Deran.'

'And where in the nine hells is that?'

'South of the Pockveld, in the lands of the old empire.'

'Well,' said Bienia. 'We had best get going then.'

CHAPTER 18

John stared at the roof of the tent. It was good to be able to lie on his back again. Whatever it was they had been slathering all over his wounds was, despite stinking of earth and rotting leaves, effective. His muscles, on the other hand, were aching. The training had been relentless. They had at least two hours training with a spear or short sword every day, and plenty of fitness training. John had never done so much running in his life. Jimmy had remarked that it was unnatural to run unless it was away from something that was trying to kill you. Their language lessons, although not physically gruelling, were mentally wearying, and John did not have much energy to think about escape or what the future held.

'Gods, I ache all over,' said Jimmy. He was sitting on his bed massaging his legs.

One of their fellow slave-soldiers chuckled and shook his head. Jimmy may have been speaking Elend, but it was obvious he was complaining.

'You northlanders find training hard?' The man was speaking Aravic. John struggled with the complex rules for tenses and gender. He was not alone; none of the non-native Aravic speakers in the spear would be winning any academic prizes for their command of the language of the old empire. They could, however, generally make themselves understood.

'I do ache,' conceded Jimmy.

'Maybe fighting spear not for you,' concluded the soldier.

'We can fight,' said John. At least, that was what he hoped he said.

The soldier nodded slowly. 'We will see. My name is Guzzai.' The man extended a hand.

John took his hand and participated in a particularly firm handshake. 'John.' He reclaimed his hand and gestured towards Jimmy. 'This Jimmy.'

'John, Jimmy.' The man rolled the names around his mouth experimentally, then barked a short laugh. 'North names funny.'

'He laughed at my name too,' said Eric.

The soldier scowled at Eric. 'Careful. You get whip speaking home words if spear-sergeant catches you.'

'You are right,' said Eric, switching to Aravic.

'Whip?' John shuddered. He had wondered why Dora had taught them that word.

Guzzai lay down on his bunk and put his hands behind his head. 'Once teacher say you understand well, you get whip if speak own words.'

'Nobody told us that,' said Jimmy.

Guzzai shrugged. 'They let you know with whip.'

'Thanks for the warning, Guzzai,' said John.

'That is okay. We are spear-comrades. Need to look after each other.'

John nodded. 'I understand.'

'Good. You northerners might live.'

Julienne sipped the smoky tasting tea and listened to the

three other language tutors exchange gossip. She had really got lucky landing a job as a language teacher. Fortunately, rather than all the Astish in one language lesson, they kept them separated into small groups. This meant more than one tutor was needed. All of them were women as teaching slaves was considered beneath all but foreigners and slaves, and all the male slaves in the war camp were being trained as warriors.

'I heard spear-captain Alfon is "playing nug-a-nug" with Bets.'

This made Julienne smile. The speaker, a young woman named Jana, had slipped into Elend to describe the activity the pair were allegedly engaging in then back into Aravic. The Aravic terms for the same pastime sounded very coarse in comparison.

'Tch, wouldn't surprise me,' said Dora in Elend.

'You think everyone is at it.' Jana had followed the older woman's cue and switched back to Elend to answer. There was nobody else nearby and they could always claim they were practicing for lessons.

'And am I wrong?' asked Dora.

'Dora, is it true you were a priestess back in Asterland?' asked Bunty. She was a large girl who maintained an astonishing level of cheerfulness despite being a slave who taught other slaves Aravic in a war-camp.

'No, girl. When I was younger, I was a mere handmaiden of Tessil, praise be his name.'

'How did you end up here?' asked Jana.

'The temple is at Kelby, by the sea———'

'Reavers,' said Jana knowingly.

Dora said nothing. There was an awkward silence as those

around the campfire thought about what reavers were known for, and what Dora would have had to endure after being taken prisoner.

Bunty managed a slight smile, took a sip from her tea and then turned to Julienne. 'Adele, where do you come from?'

'Aston,' said Julienne. Truth was easier to remember than a lie, and in this case would do just as well.

'Oooh. Did you see the King?'

'Yes.' Again, the truth.

'Is he as handsome as they say? He looks handsome on the coins.' Bunty looked around the group for affirmation.

'Yes, Bunty. He is as handsome as on the coins.'

'Did he see you?' Bunty lowered her voice to a hushed whisper. 'Did he speak to you?'

Julienne laughed, she couldn't help herself. 'No, Bunty. The King has never even looked at me, let alone spoken to me.' Now she was lying.

'I'd love to visit Aston. The riverside sounds so romantic,' said Bunty.

'The bit near my mam's house smelt dreadful in the summer,' said Julienne. And now she was back to telling the truth. She hadn't thought about her mother in a long, long time.

'Oh.' Bunty looked a bit deflated.

'Our Adele is too common for those upmarket riverside taverns,' said Dora.

'Why did you leave and come here?' asked Bunty. 'It makes no sense you being a tutor. I mean, we don't have a choice, being slaves and all, but you're free.'

Jana coughed.

'Don't be bothering Adele with your questions, Bunty,' said Dora.

'No, it's okay. I don't mind.' Julienne decided to take a calculated risk and tell a half-truth that may help her find John. She turned to Bunty and took one of her hands. 'My man is a slave-soldier here, Bunty. I'd follow him to the ends of the earth.'

Bunty's other hand flew to her mouth. 'Oh, how romantic.'

'Bloody nuts more like,' said Jana. 'No man is worth this shit.'

'I haven't found him yet. He's not in the group I teach. Perhaps one of you knows him?' Julienne put on her most pleading, desperate lover face.

'What's his name?' asked Bunty.

'John,' said Julienne.

'Sorry. No Johns in the spears I teach,' said Bunty.

Julienne looked at Jana. The woman shook her head.

Dora put down her tea and sniffed. 'John, you say?'

'Yes.'

'There's a John in Jak's spear,' said Dora.

'There is? Oh, Dora. You can get a message to him.'

'Now then. I didn't say I'd do that.'

'Come on, Dora. You've got to help,' said Bunty.

'Well...'

'Please say you will,' said Julienne.

Dora sighed and picked up her tea. She took a deliberate sip, put the cup down again, and met Julienne's gaze for a few seconds.

Julienne mustered all the forlorn helplessness she could. 'Please?'

'Tch, I may live to regret this, but I'll do it.'

Julienne grabbed the older woman's hands. They were warm from holding the cup of tea. 'Oh, thankyou thankyou thankyou.'

'Now, girl. Don't go getting all soppy on me. What do you want me to tell him?'

CHAPTER 19

'The Illians, they go to the residence.' The Aravic was awkward on John's tongue as he struggled with the phrase.

Jimmy smirked at his botched pronunciation.

Dora shook her head. 'Tch, that is no good. They do not go to the residence, they go home.'

'Sorry, Dora,' said John, unconsciously slipping back to Elend in his frustration.

Dora slapped him on the back of his head. 'In Aravic! Always Aravic.' She stood and smoothed down her skirt. 'The lesson is over. The good students will go now.' Dora pointed a boney finger at John. 'You will stay for extra teaching.'

'I will see you later,' said Jimmy in almost perfect Aravic.

'Go boil your head,' retorted John, using one of his newly learned Aravic insults.

'Good! That is better,' said Dora.

John jealously watched the two men go.

Once they were gone, Dora turned to him and said, in a low voice, 'I have a message for you.'

'A message?' John replied in Aravic.

Dora nodded. 'This is not part of the lesson. It is a message from your woman.'

'My woman?'

'She says to tell you she is here and is glad you are a soldier.'

'What?' John's mind raced. It had to be Julienne. But why was she glad that he was a slave-soldier? Then it dawned on him. He had inadvertently infiltrated the warlord's army.

'She is glad you are a soldier.' Dora shook her head. 'No, I didn't understand either. She said she will meet you outside the east latrines after the evening meal.'

'The latrines. Right.' That made sense, that was somewhere everyone had to visit. Nobody would wonder what he was doing there.

Dora laughed, misinterpreting John's expression. 'Adele is a real romantic.'

This made John smile. She couldn't help herself. She changed names like he changed trousers: at least once a month.

Dora went back to speaking Aravic. 'You can go now. The extra tuition is over.'

'Thankyou, tutor.'

Back in the spear's tent, John took Jimmy to one side and told him about Julienne.

'That's great news. She'll be able to get us out of here, right?'

'I don't think she is going to,' said John.

Jimmy looked horrified.

'At least, not right away,' added John.

'Why not?' asked Jimmy.

'I suspect she is going to tell me we are still on the mission.'

'The mission,' said Jimmy, his voice flat.

The loud voice of Guzzai cut across their conversation.

'What are you two northern fatherless bastards talking about?'

The large man approached them, a scowl on his face.

'Uh, the weather,' said John.

'Yes. It is hot. But I warned you about talking in your barbarian language,' said Guzzai.

'Yes. I apologise,' said John in Aravic.

'Don't need to apologise to me. Just don't let the spear-sergeant hear you or you will get whip.'

'The whip, right,' said John.

'Anyway. It is time for food. Come.'

John returned to his camp bed, grabbed his wooden bowl and spoon, and then followed the others outside the tent. A weasel faced man was stirring a large pot with a long wooden spoon. He joined the line of soldiers and listened to the hubbub of conversation. It was all in Aravic; John guessed that everyone wanted to avoid the whip. The accents were strong and varied, the slaves were mostly from various far-flung places. The topics of conversation were less varied and were mostly concerned with the quality of the food.

Then, he was at the front of the queue. A dollop of something brown splatted into his bowl.

'What is it?' he asked.

'Meat stew,' came the terse reply.

'What sort of meat?'

The weasel faced man shrugged.

This exchange had become quite familiar to John. He knew the 'meat stew' would not be a culinary delight. The best he could hope for was not too much gristle. He looked around for Jimmy and spotted him sitting on the ground, eating his stew and talking with Eric and Guzzai.

He sat down next to the other men and tentatively tasted his food.

'Makes you miss the food on the Banshee,' said Jimmy.

John nodded in agreement. He was moderately surprised to find himself reminiscing longingly about the rock-hard ship's biscuits on the Banshee.

'You're sailors?' asked Eric.

They hadn't spoken much about their past, except in the most vague terms. Eric knew that John was from the north of Asterland, and that was about it.

'Yes.' Jimmy looked down at the spear-sigil branded on his shoulder. 'Well, I was. I'm a soldier now, right?'

Guzzai slapped Jimmy on the back. 'Yes. You soldier now. Like all of us.'

'Does anyone know why?' asked John.

'Why what?' asked Jimmy.

'Why we're soldiers instead of farm workers or miners. What are we here for?'

'Marching, digging latrines, eating stray dogs.' Guzzai lifted a spoonful of the gristly grey stew.

Jimmy pulled a face. 'Dog?'

'I doubt it. Don't listen to him,' said John.

'How can you be so sure?' asked Jimmy.

'Can you imagine catching enough dogs to feed this lot?' John swept his arm around, indicating the whole camp.

Guzzai was still chuckling to himself swallowing another mouthful of his stew. 'Sorry. I make bad joke. It's not dog, it is probably horse.'

Jimmy shook his head. 'John's right. I'm going to stop listening to you now.'

Guzzai shrugged and continued eating.

'I heard we're heading north,' said John. This was true, he

had. Guzzai didn't need to know the source of this bit of information was the spymaster of Asterland.

'Perhaps. North, south, what does it matter?'

'Asterland is north. I was in the Asterland army. I don't want to fight my countrymen,' said Eric.

Guzzai squinted at Eric. 'You will fight or you will die. We are called slave-soldiers for a reason.'

'I'd rather be dead than a traitor,' said Eric.

John leaned forwards and put a hand on the man's arm. He switched to Elend so that Guzzai wouldn't understand him. 'Be realistic. One man won't make a difference, and we're more useful to Asterland alive.'

'Aravic!' An angry voice cut across the general hubbub of the slave-soldiers talking and eating.

John looked up and saw spear-sergeant Jak striding towards him, a cudgel in his hand.

'I am sorry, spear-sergeant,' said John.

Jak grabbed John with his free hand and pulled him roughly to his feet. 'You will speak Aravic at all times, understood?'

'I understand, spear-sergeant.'

Jak threw him to the ground and brought the cudgel down in a cracking blow to his side.

John grunted in pain and curled into a foetal position.

'If I hear you speaking your filthy northlander language again, you will be flogged. Do I make myself clear?'

'Yes, spear-sergeant.'

'Good.' Jak kicked John hard.

His side exploded with pain. John hoped he hadn't broken a rib.

Jak turned on his heel and faced the rest of the spear. The

men had all gone quiet while they watched the drama unfolding in front of them.

'That goes for all of you. Aravic. At all times.'

There was a general muttering of assent in Aravic.

Jak, apparently satisfied, stalked away leaving John to be helped up by his fellow slave-soldiers.

After finishing his bowl of the mysterious 'meat' stew, John made his way to the latrines. This was not out of the ordinary, many other slave-soldiers were making their way there after eating the stew. Once there, he hung around a tolerable distance from the stench of the latrine itself and waited for Julienne.

He almost shouted out with joy when he saw her. She was dressed in a long dress of faded red covered in so many different coloured patches that it made her look a little like a walking quilt.

He stepped towards her, a big smile on his face. 'Julienne——'

Julienne returned his smile and wrapped her arms around him, hugging him tight, and pulled him into a secluded spot between two tents.

John felt a sharp stabbing pain in his ribs. 'Aaagh!'

Julienne let go. 'Sorry. Are you hurt?'

He gingerly put a hand on his side. 'Just a little bruising. The spear-sergeant was pointing out that I should always speak Aravic. With his foot.'

'Well, we can speak Elend now. Anyone challenges us, I'm giving you a lesson.'

'Yes, I gathered you're one of the tutors.'

'Yes. I am Adele the language tutor. You need to be using that name.' Julienne wagged her finger at him like a schoolmistress admonishing an unruly child.

'Adele. Right. So, Adele, why did you want to see me?'

'Apart from missing my boyfriend, you mean?'

This brought the stupid grin back. 'Really?'

Julienne let out an exasperated sigh. 'Yes. Really. Don't let it go to your head.'

John's smile widened. He couldn't help it.

'I'm making contact with you to tell you the plan still stands. Only difference is our roles.'

'Okay.'

'See if you can find people you can trust. Be careful what you tell them, but let them know we will be helping Asterland.'

'Tell them what? I have no idea what the plan is.'

'You can't give away what you don't know.'

John sighed. 'I suppose so.'

Julienne continued, ignoring his sigh. 'We'll meet here every day and you will update me with any new information. I've told the teachers that you are my man, which should deflect any suspicion about the reason for us meeting.'

'Your man?'

'Yes. I joined up to be near you. At least, that's the story I have told them.'

John nodded. 'Right. Cover story.'

Julienne put her hand behind his head and drew him down into a kiss. John was a little surprised, but went with it.

After more than a few seconds, Julienne pulled back and winked at him. 'The best cover stories are grounded in truth.'

CHAPTER 20

Julienne sipped her wine as she watched the patrons of the tavern. She was sitting at a secluded table at the back of the tavern, far enough away from anyone so that a quiet conversation would not be overheard.

The previous day she had left a message at the dead drop for Magsi with the news that the warlord's host would be marching north to Asterland later that week. She had been surprised to find a message there for her requesting a face to face meeting the following evening. Spear-sergeant Valun had wanted to accompany her on her supposed visit to see her sick aunt, but when she described the horrible disease she was suffering from, he had decided that Julienne could go on her own, as long as she promised not to touch her aunt or let her breathe on her.

She had been waiting for half an hour when she saw Magsi enter the room. The woman was carrying a small box that had tiny holes drilled in the side. After scanning the crowded bar, she spotted Julienne and headed over.

When she arrived, Magsi put the box down onto the table and took a seat.

'Hi,' said Julienne.

'Hello, Adele,' said Magsi.

Julienne ducked her head down and tried to peer through one of the drilled holes. 'What's in the box?'

'A solution to our communication problem when the host leaves.'

'In a box?'

Magsi flipped a catch on the top of the box and lifted the lid. 'Meet Charlie and Barnet.'

Julienne looked inside the box. 'Are they... rats?'

'Yes. Macky had several pairs enchanted with a bonding spell.'

'What?'

'A local witch. They call them "magae" in Aravic.'

'And how are these two adorable fellows supposed to help us?' asked Julienne.

'Notice the collars,' said Magsi.

Julienne took another look inside the box. A little furry face looked back up at her. She saw that it was wearing a small leather collar with a metal tube attached.

'Now, I have their partners, Ethel and Kimberly. You need to get a message out, pop it in the tube and let the little fellow run free. He'll find his way back to his female, thanks to the bonding spell.'

'Ingenious,' said Julienne.

Magsi closed the lid and pushed the box towards Julienne. 'Make sure you feed them every day, and keep their box clean.'

'Right.' Julienne lifted the lid and looked at the two furry bodies inside. 'Which one is which?'

'The lighter one is Charlie, Barnet has a dark patch on the side of his nose. I'll be following the host, so the guys won't have too far to go.'

'Just be ready to get back to Asterland if you need to,' said Julienne.

Magsi nodded and clasped Julienne's hand. 'Good luck, Adele.'

Julienne smiled grimly. 'We make our own luck.'

* * *

The army was on the move. A week ago, spear-sergeant Jak had shouted them out of bed before it was light and, after a quick breakfast of cold meat stew, they had packed the tent and its contents onto several handcarts which the slave-soldiers were now pulling on the slow march north.

John coughed in a vain attempt to clear his throat of the dust being kicked up by thousands of booted feet. As well as inhaling it, he was caked in it. The dust stuck to his sweaty skin, and every fold of his clothing also had its own cache of the pernicious stuff.

The dust, the noise, and the stink of animals and unwashed men were all contributing to his misery.

'I think I've had enough of being a soldier.' Jimmy was trudging along to his left.

'Me too,' said John. He had to wonder what useful intelligence he was going to gather, stuck in the midst of the massed ranks of soldiery. He hadn't even been able to find out what meat went into the stew. Julienne hadn't contacted him since the march began. He hadn't even seen Dora; their language lessons had also stopped.

'How long until we reach Asterland?' asked Jimmy.

'It's about three inches on a map,' said John.

Jimmy managed a laugh. 'Right.'

'Asterland your home?' Guzzai was on John's right.

'That's right,' said John.

'It is good. To make war on your homeland,' said Guzzai.

John said nothing, and concentrated on putting one foot in front of the other.

'How is that good?' asked Jimmy.

Guzzai counted the reasons off on his fingers. 'You know way around. Speak language. If we lose in fight, you can pretend to be on other side.'

'You've obviously thought this through,' said Jimmy.

'Of course. If we make war on Cinnar, I will be ready.'

Guzzai tapped his nose conspiratorially.

A distant cry of 'Halt!' was barely audible over the sound of marching men. Then the column slowly came to a stop.

'What are we stopping for?' asked Jimmy.

Guzzai shrugged. 'Just be glad for rest.'

'I could do with a sit down,' said Jimmy.

'Perhaps best if we do not.' Guzzai nodded towards spear-sergeant Jak who could be seen pacing alongside them, glowering at anybody who even looked like they might be about to sit down.

The atmosphere was uneasy as the slave-soldiers started to speculate on what the hold up might be. The theories ranged from the warlord halting the column so he could relieve himself to John's particular favourite: a three-headed dragon which was demanding tribute.

It wasn't long before John saw a runner arrive and talk briefly to Jak before continuing down the line.

After the spear-sergeant had received his orders, he stood watching the men for a moment. Then, he deliberately unhooked his whip from his belt and held it by his side. 'Quiet!'

Speculation quieted to a murmur and then totally stopped under the spear-sergeant's baleful gaze.

'The time to fight has come. Remember, you fight for your spear. Form up!'

As they scrambled into some sort of order, John became aware of the other spears being organised up and down the column. This was it. He was going to be in a battle. He wondered who the enemy was?

'I wonder who we're fighting,' said Jimmy.

'Probably northlanders,' said Guzzai.

'Probably my mates,' said Eric. He was next to them in the now formed ranks of the spear.

There was a nervous tension about the slave-soldiers. John rolled his shoulders and gripped his spear.

'You going to be alright, Eric?' asked Jimmy.

'Yeah.' Eric wiped the sweat from his brow. 'Wish it wasn't so damn hot.'

'At least we don't have to wear the spear-sergeants get-up,' said Jimmy.

'You mean armour?' asked John. The spear-sergeant was wearing a fine set of hardened leather armour, and John was acutely aware that most of the spear had no armour. The more experienced soldiers, who had survived a previous battle and looted the bodies of the fallen, were wearing scavenged leather armour, and some of them even wore chainmail shirts. However, the vast majority of the men were wearing homespun woollen clothes which offered no protection from sword or arrow.

Then there was more shouting and spear-sergeant Jak got them marching double time towards whatever enemy was waiting for them. From what John could gather from his poor vantage point in the massed ranks of slave-soldiers, their spear had ended up somewhere in the centre of the warlord's army. The word passed back from the men at the front was that they had arrived at a fort.

John closed his eyes, pictured the map he and Julienne had pored over on the Banshee, and did some mental calculations. 'It must be one of the border forts.'

'If we've come up the Pock, it must be Fort Kelly. The poor bastards,' said Eric.

John thought Eric was probably correct. The Pock had been the main overland trade route from the Arann empire and the north. That was until the empire collapsed. Since then only the most well defended of trade caravans had dared to make the trip through the Pockveld. It was much safer to avoid the nomads and take your cargo by sea.

As they stood waiting in the afternoon sun, the ranks of slave-soldiers parted to allow a siege tower to be wheeled into position. This gap in the massed ranks of slave-soldiers allowed John to see the walls of the fort and the arrows which rained down on the men pushing the siege tower. The creaking rumble of the tower's wheels over the dry dusty ground was punctuated with the cries of the wounded and dying. Finally, the tower thumped into the wall of the fort. There was a shout from one of the spear-sergeants at the front of the host and, with a roar, his spear surged forward towards the base of the walls. Some of the men who charged had long ladders with them which they slammed against the wall and started climbing.

John winced as one of the ladders was pushed away and it slowly toppled backwards, men falling from it to the ground.

'Gods,' said Jimmy.

Another spear was ordered forward, the men following the others up the ladders and the siege tower. John could make out some slave-soldiers on the rightmost battlements. They had made it up the ladders and were now in bloody hand to hand combat with the fort's defenders.

And then Jak was shouting, 'Swords! Forward!' and 'Move!'

The men dropped their spears and drew their short swords. The swords would be more use in the close hand to hand fighting they would find in the fort and were much easier to carry when climbing a ladder. Fortunately, the initial torrential rain of arrows had become a light drizzle and only a couple of the slave-soldiers were cut down as they ran to the scaling ladders.

John found himself standing next to Eric near the bottom of one of the ladders. The man looked miserable.

'You okay?' John had to shout to make himself heard over the sounds of battle.

Eric looked at him and John could see the anguish in his eyes. He nodded upwards, towards the battlements. 'That's me. Up there.'

John looked away from Eric and up at the battlements. Although he felt bad about being part of an army invading Asterland, he realised it must be worse for Eric, who had actually been a soldier in one of these border forts.

Then it was their turn to climb the ladder. John went first, sheathing his sword for the climb up. They easily made it onto the battlements, stepping over the dead and dying who had paid the price to secure a foothold on top of the wall.

The defenders had been forced back into the courtyard and were slowly withdrawing to the open door of the central keep under the relentless pressure of the slave-soldiers.

'Close the doors. Close the bloody doors,' muttered Eric.

John realised the retreating Astish were not going to make it back into the keep at the same time the defenders inside decided to cut their losses and close the doors. It was too late. The slave-soldiers swarmed over the few remaining defenders, cutting them down before pushing through the half-open doors and into the keep.

'Well. That's all over,' said Eric.

'Good,' said John.

Eric shot him an acerbic look. 'Good? How is it good?'

'We don't have to fight them,' said John.

'You're right. Doors open or closed, they didn't have a chance.' Eric shaded his eyes and looked at a dark column of smoke rising from the top of the central keep. 'At least they managed to light the signal fire.'

Jimmy hoisted himself over the wall and joined them. 'Hey, did we miss all the fighting?'

'Yes,' said John.

'Thank the gods,' said Jimmy.

Eric prodded a fallen slave-soldier with his foot and shook his head. 'Don't thank them just yet. I've a feeling our turn will come soon enough.'

CHAPTER 21

Julienne gazed into the flickering flames of the campfire. The battle at Fort Kelly today had confirmed their location. They had reached the border with Asterland. Spear-sergeant Valun had told her that the few prisoners that had been taken were being transported south to be sold in the slave-markets of Olong and not drafted into the slave-soldier army as Julienne had hoped. It seemed the warlord Karvarl was not confident or stupid enough to recruit freshly defeated enemies into his army.

'Why so sad? Your man survived the battle,' said Bunty.

She realised she had been frowning and made a conscious effort to smile at the young woman. 'Yes, he did. Thank the gods.'

Dora sighed. 'It's a terrible thing to love a soldier. Doubly so a slave-soldier.' She looked at Julienne sadly. 'You'd do well to forget that young man, Adele.'

'It's not that easy, Dora.'

'Don't you listen to her, Adele. True love is always worth it,' said Bunty.

Julienne smiled at Bunty's conviction. Not so long ago she had shared Dora's point of view. Now, she was more inclined to side with Bunty.

'You're better off with someone like spear-sergeant Valun,' said Dora.

So, Dora had noticed her chats with Valun.

'I've seen the way he looks at you,' said Dora.

'Oh?' said Julienne.

'Yes. He may be a soldier, but he has more of a future than your man. He is an officer in the host.' Dora picked up a stick and started to poke at the burning logs on the fire.

'And you think he would be interested in a tutor?' Julienne was being disingenuous. She knew Valun was interested, and she had been exploiting the spear-sergeant's infatuation mercilessly.

'A tutor who is a slave? No.' Dora shook her head emphatically.

'One who is a free woman? Why not?'

Bunty put another log onto the fire. 'Oh, Dora. She loves John, don't you Adele?'

'Valun's not a bad man, and more likely to be alive next week,' said Dora.

Julienne looked sadly at Dora. 'Maybe I'll consider Valun if John—'

Bunty raised her voice, sounding quite stern. 'Don't you talk like that. Shame on you Dora, saying things like that.'

Dora stopped prodding at the fire and pointed at Julienne with the stick. 'Follow your heart if you must, but don't come crying to me if it's broken.'

'You're a terrible woman, Dora,' said Bunty.

'No, Bunty. That's okay. She is pragmatic, that's all,' said Julienne.

Dora lowered her stick and nodded. 'Pragmatic. That's what you need to be, girl.'

'I don't think it's right, that's all. Your John's nice, Adele,' said Bunty.

They slipped into silence, the only sound the crackle and pop of the campfire and the occasional sound of rough male voices in the distance.

'Well. I think I'll be off to bed,' said Dora.

'Goodnight, Dora,' said Julienne.

'G'night,' said Bunty.

Bunty and Julienne sat staring into the flames for a few minutes after the older woman had left.

It was Julienne broke the silence.

'Do you miss Asterland?'

'Yes, of course. I'm kind of nervous to be going back. As part of an invading army, I mean.'

Julienne nodded. 'It's not as if you're doing any fighting.'

'No, I suppose not. I just wish—' Bunty stopped and looked around nervously before continuing in a whisper. 'I wish I could do something. You know?'

Julienne looked at Bunty and was surprised to see a steely determination in her face. Maybe Bunty could be of use?

'I just, oh damn it, I hate what is happening.' Bunty clenched her fists.

'Maybe you can,' said Julienne.

Bunty unclenched her fists and looked at Julienne in surprise. 'What?'

'Maybe you can help Asterland.'

'But how?'

'The same way I am.'

Bunty's eyes widened even more. 'You? You're helping Asterland?'

Julienne nodded. 'I try to find out where the army is going. What their plans are.'

'A spy? Really?' Bunty put a hand on Julienne's arm.

Julienne covered Bunty's hand with her own. 'You have to promise not to tell anyone.'

Bunty glanced to her left and right before answering. 'Of course. This is so exciting, Adele.'

'And dangerous. Only agree to help if you are sure.'

She felt Bunty's grip on her arm tighten slightly. 'I'm sure. What do I have to do?'

Julienne leaned in close. 'Get close to an officer and find things out.'

'Close? You mean...'

'I mean the way I am with spear-sergeant Valun.'

Comprehension dawned on Bunty's face. 'You've been finding things out from him.'

'Yes.'

'But what about John? Are you using him too?'

'John is different,' said Julienne.

'Oh, good.' Bunty's smile seemed genuine.

'Do you think you can do it?'

Bunty looked thoughtful. 'There is spear-sergeant Dal. He sometimes tries talking to me at meal times.'

'Yes, I'd noticed. Spear-sergeant Dal then. Just get him interested, no questioning him.'

'I thought that was the whole point?'

'Yes, but you need to get him to trust you first. Just work on that.'

'Okay,' said Bunty hesitantly.

'Once you have him wrapped around your finger, I'll tell you what to ask him, then we can compare notes.'

'You want me to take notes?' asked Bunty.

'Only mental ones. We really don't want anyone knowing what we're up to. Which brings me to my next point. Don't tell anyone, not even Dora.'

There was a loud pop from the fire that made Bunty visibly jump. 'Not Dora?'

'Not anyone,' said Julienne.

Bunty nodded. 'I can do that. I mean, I won't do that.'

'Good. Now, get some sleep, you'll be wanting to look fresh and eager for the spear-sergeant.'

CHAPTER 22

The rain cascaded down in an unrelenting torrent onto Port Denly. The wind drove lashing sheets of water along the streets, soaking the few hardy souls who had ventured outside. The city had mostly recovered from the occupation by the dwarven clans and day-to-day life had returned to normal. A handful of dockworkers braving the rain to load the 'Pageant', a two-masted trading ship, were the first on the shore to notice the four ships on the horizon. It did not take long for word to spread and a crowd of onlookers soon gathered on the docks, curious about the identity of the approaching vessels.

Barnaby, the skipper of the small cutter carving its way through the rough seas towards the oncoming ships, was also curious, and a little nervous. The naval blockade of Port Denly was still fresh in his mind and his fears were being fed by the possibility that this was a new rebel fleet.

Barnaby wiped the water from the end of his spyglass and looked through it at the lead ship. He lowered the spyglass and blinked away the rainwater that was blurring his vision, then took a second look. No, he had been right the first time. The crew were dwarves.

'Captain?' Jason, his first officer was waiting patiently

beside him, the rain battering him as he held the ship's rail with one hand and his tricorn hat in place with the other.

'Bloody dwarves,' said Barnaby.

'Dwarves, sir? Is it another invasion?'

'Bring us about!' shouted Barnaby. They had to get back and raise the alarm.

Lord Mayhew wasted no time in organising a suitable welcome for the approaching dwarven flotilla. He didn't know what had prompted the clans to return to Port Denly, but he wasn't about to let the dwarves of the Silver Hills retake his city. It was, of course, possible that the dwarves on the four ships were friendly, but turning up unannounced and in force suggested more hostile intentions.

The dockworkers had stacked barrels and crates along the waterfront, then retreated to the safety of the city. Behind this makeshift barricade crouched the few crossbowmen that remained in the city garrison. Lord Mayhew hoped they would be enough. The bulk of his men had gone south to join the King's army in the fight against the rebel Lord Ponder and his allies.

Away from the barricades, in one of the side streets, Lord Mayhew waited with two dozen men-at-arms, ready to intercept the invaders when they landed. There was a cry of alarm and he shifted his attention to the approaching vessels. A strange cloud was rising from the prow of the lead ship. The dwarven crew started lowering rowing boats into the water as the cloud started to move towards the shore.

Lord Mayhew gave an involuntary gasp of astonishment as the cloud got closer and resolved into a swarm of tiny winged figures. 'What in the gods is that?'

'Feck!' 'Arse!' 'Buggerit!' – a background babble of swearing accompanied the swarm as it streaked over the heads of the crossbowmen and into the city. A couple of the men fired optimistically into the swarm, but the bolts passed through without hitting any of the tiny targets.

'Hold your fire!' shouted Lord Mayhew. He turned to the chainmail clad man standing next to him. 'Captain, send some men into the city. Find out what those—those whatever they were are up to.'

'Fairies I think, my lord.'

'Fairies, right.' Mayhew looked his captain up and down. 'Why are you still standing there? Go!'

'Yes, my lord.'

The captain hurried away to do his bidding.

The rowing boats were now approaching the docks. They were overflowing with short figures waving wickedly sharp knives and axes. Lord Mayhew frowned. They did not look like clan dwarves. They were stockier than dwarves from the silver hills and had low beetling eyebrows above their glaring malevolent eyes. They wore black chainmail shirts and simple cloth caps dyed a vivid scarlet.

There was a cry of 'Open fire!' from the sergeant-at-arms by the barricade and a volley of crossbow bolts swept across the rowing boats. Several of the occupants were hit, and either fell into the sea or amongst their comrades who then pushed them out of the boat and into the water. This initial volley was followed by more ragged fire as the men loaded and fired their crossbows as fast as they could.

Then, the rowing boats reached the docks, and the redcaps sprang out of the boats and onto the quayside, charging the barricades while shouting coarse battle-cries.

Lord Mayhew drew his sword and held it aloft. 'With me!'

He led the men-at-arms forward to the barricades nearest the charging redcaps while the crossbowmen fell back, away from the attackers, moving behind the shield of the men-at-arms.

The redcaps swarmed up the barricades, hurling themselves over the top. Mayhew raised his shield and took the thumping impact of one of the invaders.

A curved dagger flashed around the side of his shield, its edge dripping with a thick black liquid. Mayhew violently shoved his shield forwards and down, throwing the redcap backwards onto the ground. His foe sprung back to his feet and glared at Mayhew.

Mayhew adjusted his grip on his shield, lifting it back in place. 'Come on then. What are you waiting for, you bastard?'

The redcap smiled disconcertingly. 'You die now.' Its eyes darted to Mayhew's right and back again.

The sound of metal on metal and a gasp came from Mayhew's right and he risked a look away from the figure in front of him. A redcap was kneeling on the prone man-at-arms by his side and had just slid its black knife through his chain gorget. The redcap turned his head and looked at him, teeth bared in a primal snarl.

Mayhew took a step back and moved his shield around, trying to keep it between himself and the two redcaps.

The sounds of battle seemed to fade away as they looked at him, knives ready. Then they exploded into motion, simultaneously leaping at him, a shrill battle-cry on their lips. Mayhew batted one aside with his shield and thrust his sword at the second. The blade tore into the redcap's jerkin and sprayed bright red blood along Mayhew's arm. It only slowed the redcap's leap slightly and Mayhew had the wind knocked out of him as the creature smashed into his chest, throwing him backwards. As he crashed to the floor, Mayhew lost his grip on his sword and it skittered away across the cobblestones.

The fetid smell of rotting meat filled his nostrils as the redcap leaned over him. 'You die. Now.'

He felt a sharp pain in his neck and suddenly gasped, fighting to breathe. He heard a bubbling noise as he struggled to draw air into his lungs. The redcap leaned on his knife and Mayhew felt the pressure mount on his neck in a searing agony.

Mayhew gave one last gurgling gasp, then fell silent, his lifeless eyes staring up at the warped grinning face of his killer as he gleefully sawed his knife back and forth.

Barnaby watched aghast as Lord Mayhew was cut down, overwhelmed by the savagery of the redcaps. The crossbowmen were starting to run, making for the keep in the centre of the city.

'Bollocks to this. I'm out of here,' said Jason.

Jason was right, this was no place for a pair of naval men like themselves.

Barnaby shook his first officer's hand. 'Where will you go?'

'Got a sister in Estershire. I reckon I'll go there.'

Barnaby nodded. 'Well, good luck.'

Jason threw one last salute at his captain and then turned and ran away, up the alley.

Barnaby took a final look at the melee on the quayside, then followed suit, heading for his lodgings on Dial street. He needed to pick up a few things before leaving the city. He had just passed the 'Lonesome Badger' tavern, when something thumped into his shoulder making him stagger to one side. He looked up and saw three diminutive fluttering fairies each carrying a large rock.

A fourth fairy, whose hands were empty, was pointing down at Barnaby. 'See if you can hit his fecking head.'

One of the fairies let go of the rock he was carrying and it plummeted down towards Barnaby. He dashed forwards as the rock clattered on the cobblestones behind him and ducked through the tavern doorway. Inside, was bedlam. A number of fairies had found their way in and discovered the bar.

Several patrons were hiding behind tables flipped on their sides. One of them, a portly balding man, noticed him standing in the doorway. 'Get down!'

Barnaby hastily threw himself to the floor as an empty beer bottle arced towards him from the direction of the bar. He threw his arms over his head as it smashed against the wall, showering him with shards of broken glass.

With a tinkle of falling glass, Barnaby lowered his arms, then scrambled over to a nearby table joining a pretty dark haired young woman in a rather low cut black and red dress.

He cautiously peered over the top of the table and then hurriedly ducked as another bottle whistled over his head accompanied by a cheer from the direction of the bar.

'Stay down,' said the woman.

Barnaby looked at the gap between himself and the tavern door. If he attempted to cross it, he would be bombarded with flying glassware. 'How am I supposed to get out?'

'Maybe they'll run out of bottles,' hazarded the woman.

Barnaby turned his full attention to his new companion. She was wearing plenty of charcoal eyeshadow and bright red lip paint.

'Maybe,' said Barnaby.

'Sylvie.' The woman held out a hand. Her nails had been painted the same red colour as her lips.

Barnaby took her hand, it was cold and damp. 'Captain Barnaby Twintle,' he said.

Another bottle flew over their heads and bounced off of the wall, hit the floor and rolled across the floor.

'Well, Captain Barnaby Twintle. Would you be able to help get a lady out of here?'

'I would, except there are more of the buggers outside,' said Barnaby.

'Hmm.' A frown briefly wrinkled her delicate features, then she smiled. 'Well then, Barnaby, would you like to come upstairs with me?'

Barnaby blushed. 'I don't think we have time.'

Sylvie giggled. 'No silly, not like that. We can stop being bottle target practice, over there.' She pointed at an open doorway leading to a stairway up. There was plenty of open space with no cover between it and them. Another bottle bounced off the wall and clattered along the floor to their left.

'I still don't see——'

'We pick up the table and walk it over,' said Sylvie.

'Oh. I see. Right.'

They grabbed a table leg each, lifted and started to shuffle over towards the stairway. Bottles continued to arc over their heads and thump into the tabletop accompanied by the cheering and swearing of the fairies. When the end of the table butted up against the wall, Barnaby grabbed Sylvie's hand and pulled her through the opening and up the stairs, onto the landing and into one of the rooms, before slamming the door shut behind them.

Sylvie smiled at Barnaby. 'Thank you.' She looked down.

Barnaby followed her gaze and saw they were still holding hands. He let go. 'Sorry.'

'I can tell you're a captain. Very strong and commanding.'

Sylvie ran a hand down his arm.

'Please, don't.'

Sylvie sighed. 'We may be trapped up here for a while. Until those fairies leave the bar at least.'

'Maybe we can climb down.' Barnaby opened the window shutters. There were columns of smoke rising into the air all over the city and he could hear distant sounds of fighting. Three winged figures flew into view and stopped, hovering above the road. One of them noticed him and pointed. Barnaby hurriedly closed the shutters. 'Maybe not.'

'Then we're stuck here. Together.' Sylvie sat down on the bed and patted the bedclothes next to her. 'Sit down, captain Barnaby Twintle, tell me about yourself.'

Barnaby hesitated, then sat down next to the woman. 'Well, I am—was a captain in the harbour patrol.'

The next morning, Barnaby woke with a start, momentarily forgetting the events of the previous day. He turned his head and saw Sylvie, sleeping peacefully, her eye make-up smeared across her cheek. Had they? He shook his head to clear the fog of sleep. No, they had not had sex. They had stayed up late into the night, listening to the city in chaos outside and talking about their lives. He hadn't meant to, but he had told her his life story, how he had married young, his pride at becoming a captain, his anguish and sorrow when his wife and child died in childbirth. It all came tumbling out.

She had listened to him patiently until he had run out of things to say. Then, she had told him her story. He had almost cried while Sylvie told him about her childhood. The daughter of a prostitute, she had been enlisted into the profession at an early age. It had made him want to exact a bloody revenge on the men who were responsible. Sylvie had placed a hand on his arm and told him that he was sweet, but it was just the way things were. It hadn't made him feel any better about it.

He got out of bed and opened the window shutters. The morning sun was starting to peek over the rooftops and he could hear the strident sound of gulls squabbling over food. There didn't seem to be any fairies in the air, perhaps they would be gone from the bar too.

'Barnaby?'

He turned away from the window and saw Sylvie looking at him while rubbing the sleep from her eyes.

'I think they've gone. Let's go,' said Barnaby.

Soon, the two of them were slowly walking down the stairs, listening intently for any sign of the fairies. When they got to the bar, it was unoccupied. The devastation from the night before was complete. There was a sea of broken glass and puddles of beer all across the floor, and the bar itself looked like it had been on fire at one end – the wood was blackened and cracked.

'Good, they've left,' said Barnaby.

'Then, so should we,' said Sylvie.

Barnaby nodded and led the way out. The street was eerily quiet. Normally at this time in the morning, it would be filled with people all going about their business, but there wasn't a soul around.

'Where is everyone?' asked Sylvie, echoing his thoughts.

'I don't know, but I don't think we should hang around. The east gate is closest, let's go.'

They were at the the junction of Candle Street and Jay Street when Sylvie suddenly stopped, put a hand on his arm and said, 'Did you see that?'

'See what?'

Sylvie pointed to a rooftop. 'I thought I saw something. Up there.'

'Probably just a pigeon. We don't have time to waste, come on.'

He heard a gurgling laugh from behind him and saw Sylvie's eyes widen.

'Captain Barnaby!'

He spun on his heel and saw one of the creatures that he had seen fighting the soldiers yesterday. Yellow eyes glared out at him from under the peak of a blood-red cap.

'Shit,' said Barnaby.

The creature smiled evilly. 'Now, that's not nice, is it Burr?'

A second redcap emerged from the shadows of an alleyway. 'They don't seem pleased to see us Spike.'

Barnaby took a step back, putting his body between the redcaps and Sylvie.

'This one called this other one a captain. Will they do, do you think?' asked the one called Spike.

'I think they will. You lucky people get to meet the King.' Spike unrolled a net made of thick rope.

'The King?' asked Sylvie.

Burr grabbed the other end of the net and the pair advanced on Barnaby and Sylvie.

'Run!' shouted Barnaby.

They turned, ready to run away from the menace of Burr and Spike only to see another pair of redcaps behind them both holding short black knives.

Then, the net was over their heads and they were dragged struggling to the floor.

Sylvie pulled at the ropes of the net in vain. 'Let us go!'

'Only one place you're going, my lovely, and that's to see King Oberon,' said Spike.

CHAPTER 23

Barnaby and Sylvie were taken to the keep in the centre of Port Denly and then separated. The redcaps proceeded to kick and punch Barnaby for a while until they lost interest, leaving him gasping on the floor of one of the cells beneath the keep. Since then, the only thing marking the passing of time was the irregular delivery of bread and water into the cell, and he had begun to lose track of how many days had passed. The walls and floor were damp, the cold had seeped into Barnaby's bones, and he was hungry and feeling truly wretched. It was all some horrible nightmare that he couldn't wake from.

A key rattled in the lock. It must be time for food again, he thought dully.

'Oi, get up.' The redcap's voice was gruff and cruel.

Barnaby stayed where he was.

'I said, get up.' This was punctuated by sudden pain as a boot connected with his ribs.

Barnaby heaved himself to his feet.

'That's better, now get moving, and don't try any funny business.'

He hesitantly exited the cell, blinking as his eyes adjusted to the flickering torch light in the corridor.

'Go right 'til I tell you to stop or I'll hit you with my stick.'

The stick in question was black and studded with rusty iron nails. Barnaby obeyed, tripping over his own feet as he stumbled down the corridor. He hadn't walked anywhere for a while, and his legs felt rubbery. He had a little trouble with the stairs, but managed to get to the top without the redcap delivering the threatened beating. He entered the large entrance hall. Sunlight was streaming through narrow windows set high in the walls and his eyes had to adjust again to a new level of brightness.

Another redcap approached him and he felt them grab his arms. He didn't resist. He felt his eyes close and his head loll forwards. His head felt light.

He was vaguely aware of voices. 'Is it dead?'

'Nah. It's resting, look.'

A jab in his bruised ribs jolted him to his senses. 'Stop, please.'

One of the redcaps grinned triumphantly. 'See?'

'Good. We best take him to see the King.'

Barnaby let himself be taken into the banqueting hall. He had been here before, during the harvest feast last year. He had been proud to be invited there by Lord Mayhew. He realised he had last seen his Lord on the docks, falling under a swarm of redcaps. He groaned.

'You be quiet 'till you're talked to.'

A large throne was at one end of the hall. Barnaby did not remember it being there during his last visit. He would have remembered it. It looked like it was made of living trees, the legs the trunks and the back made of their branches wrapped around each other. The flagstones around its base were tilted at crazy angles as if it had thrust its way through from underneath.

The figure sitting on the throne exuded an aura of regal

power. A thin silver circlet sat on top of long blonde hair, and his vivid violet eyes seemed to see into Barnaby's soul.

'Approach.'

One of the redcaps shoved him in the back and he lurched forward. As he got closer to what he assumed was the king the redcaps had spoken of, he became aware of a woman by the throne. She was beautiful, dressed in a swirl of sky-blue scarves and a long, flowing skirt. He looked again. Was that Sylvie?

'Barnaby.' The King stood up and walked towards him. He was tall, and his ears were pointed.

Barnaby took an involuntary step back.

'The correct response is "My King". Can you try that for me, Barnaby?'

Barnaby couldn't stop looking at the strange man's eyes. 'I...'

'Yes?'

Barnaby felt the words come, almost unbidden. 'Yes, my King.'

The man said something in a strange, musical tongue and Barnaby knew that he would do anything for his King.

'Do you remember Lady Sylvie?' asked Oberon.

Barnaby looked at Sylvie. He remembered. 'Yes, my King.'

'Good. You and Lady Sylvie will join my court as Lord and Lady and advise me about this realm.'

'I...' Barnaby was overwhelmed with gratitude and love for Oberon. 'Thank you, my King.'

Oberon gave Sylvie a lingering kiss, then turned and embraced Barnaby.

'Do not disappoint me, Lord Barnaby,' Oberon whispered in his ear before releasing him.

Barnaby knew that he would rather die than fail his King.

'Burr and Spike, you and your redcaps will obey the new Lord and Lady.'

The two redcaps looked surly.

'You will obey Lord Barnaby and Lady Sylvie as if the orders come from me. Do you understand?'

'Yes, my King,' said Burr and Spike in unison.

CHAPTER 24

Once they left the foothills of the Spiky mountains, the dwarves and Pockle descended into the county of Estershire. Following the roads that wound their way around the hills of Estershire, they made good time, buying food from the sheep farms they passed on their way. After several days of walking, they crested a hill overlooking the river Treal, the unofficial border between the north and south of Asterland. The city of Sike straddled the river, covering the valley in a sea of rooftops.

'I've never been this far south,' said Bienia.

'I've never been away from Saltrock,' said Neave.

Pockle was sitting on Brynhild's shoulder, gently bobbing up and down as she walked. 'If it's a fecking contest, I'd never been out of the Spiky mountains until I ran into that old git, Snorri.'

Hevac snorted back a laugh. 'Can we all agree that none of you are well travelled?'

'And you are, Hevac?' asked Brynhild.

Bienia hastily changed the subject. Brynhild and the others didn't need to know about Maena just yet. 'We should try to get a coach south when we get to the city.'

'A coach? Are you sure?' asked Brynhild.

'Horses aren't that bad when they're pulling a coach,' said Bienia.

'If you say so,' said Brynhild dubiously.

'Trust me, if we want to get to our destination before the end of this year, we need to take a coach.'

'And where's our destination?' asked Brynhild.

'I told you. The Tomb of Emperor Yavin,' Bienia said.

'To find a dagger called Feybane,' said Brynhild.

'You got it,' said Bienia.

'We all have it. Can we go now?' asked Hevac.

'Sure, of course,' said Bienia.

Maena had to admit, Sike was big and busy. But it was not as impressive as the cities of the ancient Arann empire. The architecture was nowhere near as regal or impressive; there was a distinct lack of marble columns.

The bed in her room at the inn was very welcome. Weeks spent sleeping under the stars, while sounding romantic, was as tiring as it was uncomfortable. She lay back on the bed holding her arm up and inspected the back of Hevac's hand. It seemed very hairy. She wondered if she should wax them.

'*Don't you dare!*'

Maena chuckled.

'*I don't see what's funny.*'

Maena thoughtfully stroked her beard. 'Maybe I should shave everything off?'

Hevac said nothing, but she could feel a shocked silence.

'Oh, stop worrying. I'm not going to shave anything.'

'*Good.*'

'Except, maybe...' Maena lifted the waistband of her trousers and peered down.

'*Please, don't.*'

There was a knock at the door. Maena stood up and opened it, a smirk still on her face. Bienia was there.

'I've sorted out a coach. We're on one leaving tomorrow morning. You'll have to be up early, so I recommend an early night,' said Bienia.

Maena nodded and started to push the door closed.

Bienia stuck her foot in the way. 'I think we need to talk.'

'We do?'

'Yes. we do.' Bienia squeezed past and into the room. Maena needed to not be alone with Bienia right now. She could feel a gentle pressure south of her waistband as this vessel reacted to physical contact with the female dwarf and she wasn't entirely confident that she would be able to ignore it given enough temptation.

'What about?' Maena stepped back, closed the door and dropped her hands nonchalantly in front of the offending part of her vessel's anatomy.

'About how long you're planning on staying inside Hevac.'

'I was planning on as long as it takes.'

'Not good enough,' said Bienia.

'I don't see how saying that will change anything. I need another willing vessel, and I don't see many around here. Do you?'

'There's me,' said Bienia quietly.

'*What?*'

'What?'

'I said—'

'I heard what you said.'

'You can do that right? Transfer into me?'

If she did, she would be rid of this vessel and with Bienia again. The thought was strangely comforting. She went to her bag, pulled out her dagger and stood looking at the depiction of a pair of rutting dogs that had been worked into the leather of the sheath. She smiled to herself. It had been Andraste's.

'Maena?'

'Yes, Bienia. I will do it.'

'*No!*'

Would Hevac prefer her to occupy Neave?

'*I cannot let you take Bienia.*'

'I can do this only if you are willing.'

'*I am not!*'

'It will be like last time, right?'

Maena hesitated. She really wanted to be in control, not relegated to the back of Bienia's mind. 'Sort of.'

'What do you mean, sort of?'

'I will be the dominant personality.'

'No way,' said Bienia.

'I am only willing to do this if I am in control. Do you want me out of your goatherd or not?'

Bienia held Maena's gaze. 'I do. But, no way am I letting you take over.'

'*Hah. She will not do it. I will not do it.*'

'Then, I am afraid we are at an impasse.'

'*Good.*'

'Maena, I...' Bienia stepped closer and Maena could smell sweat. Her eyes were drawn to the two undone buttons at the top of the shieldmaiden's shirt. She shifted her gaze up to Bienia's perfect brown eyes.

Bienia's eyes flicked downwards, avoiding Maena's, and then she frowned. 'Do you have an erection?'

Maena looked down. The fabric of Hevac's trousers was tented outwards.

'*I'm sorry. She has that effect on me.*'

'That is...' Maena looked up and into Biena's eyes. 'That is this vessel.'

'Are you in there Hevac?' Bienia held Maena's gaze.

It was no good. She couldn't take this any more. Maena leaned in and kissed Bienia, quickly, on the lips.

'Hevac,' whispered Bienia.

'*Wait. What are you doing?*'

And then they were kissing. It felt good, natural, and Maena felt a thrill as Hevac's desire overtook her and Bienia's hands wrapped around her waist.

'*No, no, no. This is wrong!*'

The desire suddenly withered away, and Maena pushed Bienia away, pulling out of the kiss.

Bienia dropped her hands to her sides. 'Hevac?' she said in a small voice.

'No,' said Maena. 'Sorry.'

'Damn it, Maena.' Bienia's eyes were damp.

'Maybe it would be best if you kept your distance,' said Maena.

'We get this done, and then you're out of Hevac?'

'You are going to have to trust me.'

Bienia stared at Maena for a few moments. 'Do I have a choice?'

'Not really, no.'

CHAPTER 25

John concentrated on putting one foot in front of the other. He was beginning to wonder what good he was doing the Asterland war effort. He had not seen Julienne for a couple of days and, despite knowing she can look after herself, was beginning to get a little worried. He listened as the others talked.

'I will be glad when we get where the warlord has decided we are going,' said Guzzai.

'Wherever that is,' said Jimmy.

'Aston,' said Eric. 'This is the road to Aston.'

'Oh,' said Jimmy. 'Makes sense.'

'What is Aston?' asked Guzzai.

John looked up from his feet and saw Eric looking incredulously at Guzzai. 'Seriously?'

'What? What did I say?' asked Guzzai.

'It's the capital city,' said John.

'Oh.' Guzzai shrugged.

'I don't think we'll get there without a fight,' said Eric.

'Good. I am bored of walking,' said Guzzai.

That evening, after the army had made camp, dug latrines, and served up some gristly meat stew, the four comrades were sitting by a campfire. Guzzai was gulping ale from a bottle which he had managed to liberate from a farmhouse and somehow keep hidden from the spear-sergeant.

He belched and handed the bottle to John. 'I go piss now.'

Once Guzzai had left, Eric spoke in a low, urgent tone. 'We need to escape. Get back to the Astish army.'

Jimmy looked left and right before hunkering down. 'Are you crazy? They'll flog us raw.'

'Only if they catch us,' said Eric.

'Let's not be hasty,' said John.

'Not be hasty? We've been in Asterland for over a week.'

'We are more use to the King here,' said John.

Eric sat up straight, his voice rising. 'More use? In an enemy army? Are you deranged?'

'Keep it down,' hissed Jimmy.

'Eric.' John paused. Should he tell him? Julienne had asked him to recruit people he could trust, and Eric was a countryman. 'We, me and Jimmy, didn't end up in the warlord's army by accident.'

'We didn't? News to me,' said Jimmy.

'Well, I suppose it was a little accidental,' conceded John.

Eric frowned. 'What are you talking about?'

'I was sent here on a mission,' said John.

'Mission? To do what?'

Jimmy chuckled. 'I've been wondering that myself.'

John looked from one man to the other. 'I'm with a spy who is running the operation, so I'm not that sure myself.' Now that he said it out loud, it sounded awful.

'So, you don't know why you're here,' said Eric.

'I didn't say that. I'm here to defend Asterland.'

Eric shook his head. 'Funny way of going about it. Being part of an invading army.'

'Look, all I'm saying is, she said stay in the army, so I'm staying. If you want to help me with whatever I'm told to do, then that would be more use to King Stephen than trying to desert.'

'I don't know,' said Eric.

'Why the serious faces?' Guzzai was back from the latrine.

'We've run out of beer.' John held up the bottle, then gulped down the rest of its contents as fast as he could. He wiped the back of his hand across his mouth and belched loudly.

'Well, shit. It's a good thing your good friend Guzzai has second one hidden, yes?' Guzzai held up another bottle, then pulled the cork from the neck with a pop.

'Nice one,' said Jimmy.

A woman's voice came from the shadows. 'Hope you're saving some of that for me.'

John turned, straining his fire blinded eyes peering into the darkness.

A woman stepped into the circle of firelight. She was wrapped in a loose fitting, dusty brown robe with the hood up. She pulled back the hood to reveal Julienne, her smile showing through the grit and grime from the trail.

'Adele,' said John, being careful to use her currently adopted name.

'Hi.' Jimmy waved.

'Do you boys mind if I have a quick word with my man?'

Guzzai smiled suggestively. 'A word? Or—'

John hastily interrupted the slave-soldier. 'Come on, Adele, we can talk away from this lot,' said John.

Julienne took his hand and led him away to a shadowy secluded spot between two tents. 'Have you had a chance to talk to them?'

'I was just doing that.'

'And?'

'Jimmy is, of course, with us. I think Eric will be too.'

'What about the big guy? He'd be useful in a scrape,' said Julienne.

'Guzzai? I don't know. He's not Astish.'

'But he's a slave, right? How much loyalty does he have to his masters?'

John thought for a moment. 'None. He's a bit of a pragmatist.'

'Sound him out,' said Julienne.

'You sure?'

'For what I have planned? Yes.'

'Do I get to know what you have planned?' asked John.

'It's on a need to know basis, and right now you don't need to know.'

John started to sigh but was interrupted by a kiss from Julienne.

'That's on account,' said Julienne.

'So, what do I tell Guzzai?'

'About what?'

'About what it is I'm asking him to do.'

'Tell him you are going to betray your masters and strike a blow for Asterland,' said Julienne.

'I'm not sure he'll go for that.'

'Tell him there will be a bag of gold and his freedom waiting for him in Aston.'

'Now that he might go for.'

'Good.' Julienne kissed him again. 'Go bond with your comrades.'

John rejoined the others at the campfire. Guzzai had a knowing smile on his face. 'That was quick. Even for a northerner.'

'Any of that beer left?' asked John.

'You want more, after you drank the last one?' asked Guzzai.

'Here.' Jimmy got to his feet and passed John the bottle. 'I've had enough anyway.' He stood yawned and stretched his arms theatrically. 'Time for sleep.'

'You're right. We probably have more marching tomorrow,' said Eric.

Once Eric and Jimmy had left, John sat down next to Guzzai and handed him the beer.

Guzzai shook the bottle next to his ear, smiling at the sound of sloshing ale inside. 'At least you bastards left me some.'

'Guzzai, can we talk?'

Guzzai laughed. 'What are we doing now?'

John quickly checked that nobody was in earshot. 'Do you like being a slave?'

'That is a stupid question. Men are meant to be free.'

'So you would like to be free?'

'Yes, of course.'

'If you help me to help the King of Asterland, he would free you.'

Guzzai leant in close to John and whispered, 'That is dangerous talk.'

'It's not just talk,' said John.

Guzzai looked at John, steadily, appraisingly. 'No?'

'No. Help us and you'll be free.'

Guzzai sucked air through his teeth. 'It is a risky business.'

'Did I mention the King will give you gold?'

'Why would he give a simple slave-soldier gold?'

'All soldiers of Asterland are paid gold. They aren't slaves.' John was exaggerating a bit here. Their wages were almost exclusively paid in silver and copper.

'A paid soldier of Asterland.' Guzzai's face broke into a broad grin. 'Sounds better than a slave-soldier of the warlord.'

'Then you are in?'

'As long as it doesn't look like you'll get me killed? Yes.'

Later, inside the tutors tent, Julienne and Bunty had retired early to discuss what Bunty had discovered from spear-sergeant Dal. Disappointingly, she had discovered nothing that Julienne did not already know.

'Bunty, check outside will you?' asked Julienne.

Bunty lifted the flap for a moment and peered outside. 'Nobody about.'

Julienne moved to a wooden box near her bedroll and lifted the lid to reveal two brown haired rats, who stood on their hind legs squeaking as she threw in a limp cabbage leaf and half a carrot. Both of them were wearing leather collars.

'I don't know why you keep those things. I hate rats,' said Bunty.

'They make good pets.'

Julienne picked up one of the rats and stroked its head murmuring to it softly. She then slid a rolled up a piece of parchment into a small metal tube tied to the rat's collar.

'What's that?' asked Bunty.

'Don't you worry about that. Or tell anyone.' Julienne clutched the rat with one hand while she replaced the lid on the box with her other. Then, she stood up and walked past Bunty, towards the tent flap.

'Eh! Get that thing away from me!'

Julienne ignored her, knelt by the tent flap and released the rat. 'Go on Charlie. Find your girl.'

The rat turned to look at her, twitched its whiskers and then scampered off into the darkness.

CHAPTER 26

The dwarves had made good time on the main trade road that ran south from Estershire, through the towns of eastern Asterland and into the Pockveld. Now, the farms and woodland of southern Asterland had given way to the arid plains of the Pockveld. They had stopped at the side of the road for lunch when they spotted a cloud of dust in the distance to the west.

Bienia shaded her eyes and contemplated the long, low cloud of dust on the horizon.

'That looks like an army,' said Brynhild.

'I agree. And quite a large one judging from the amount of dust,' said Bienia.

'Do you think it's King Stephen's?' asked Brynhild.

'Maybe. They shouldn't be this far south though, we've already passed the border forts, and last I heard the King was sorting out things up north.'

'Irrelevant,' said Hevac.

'Pockle, can you fly over and get a closer look?' asked Brynhild.

'Sure thing. I'll be right fecking back babe.' Pockle flitted up from his perch on Brynhild's shoulder and shot off in the direction of the dust cloud.

'Did he just call you babe?' asked Bienia.

Brynhild's face flushed. 'I don't see what's wrong with that.'

'I believe our shieldmaiden companion has deepened the fairy-bond with that vermin,' said Hevac.

'What is the deal with this fairy-bond?' asked Bienia.

'Fairy-bond? I don't even know what one of those is,' said Brynhild.

'It's an ancient magic,' said Hevac.

'Perverted magic.' Neave glared at Brynhild as if daring her to say something.

Brynhild shrugged. 'I'm not afraid of a bit of perversion. Makes the world go around. That's what I say.'

'Clearly,' said Hevac drily.

Bienia scratched her head. 'So it's playing nug-a-nug with a fairy?'

'More magical than mere sex,' said Hevac.

'I don't know. I find sex quite magical,' said Brynhild.

'The fairy-bond is one formed over time. It is a deep and spiritual connection between dwarf and fairy.'

'Bloody deep and perverted, more like,' said Neave.

Brynhild subtly shifted her stance, resting her hand easily on her sword hilt. 'You got a problem, Neave?'

'I'm sure Neave didn't mean it,' said Bienia. The last thing she needed was Brynhild injuring Hevac's sister. Although she was also tempted to punch the aspirant in the face, she needed this little group pulling together, for now at least.

'She is right though. It is revoltingly perverse magic,' said Hevac.

'You want some as well goat-boy? I've got plenty of butt-kicking to go round.'

Bienia put a hand on Brynhild's sword arm. 'Bryn, please.'

Brynhild shot Bienia an angry look. 'Tell your boyfriend to keep a civil tongue in his head, Bee.'

Bienia hoped Maena would have the sense not to provoke Brynhild further. 'Hevac, please.'

Hevac held up his hands. 'Sorry, sorry. I promise not to mention it again.'

Pockle landed on Brynhild's shoulder, steadying himself with a hand on the top of her head. 'Not mention what?'

'It doesn't matter,' said Bienia. 'What did you see?'

'A crap-ton of men on horses, and a lot of guys with spears and stuff. All heading north.'

'But who are they? Any banners?'

'Yes, but there was a bit of a theme of fangs, claws, and curved swords. They didn't look fecking Astish,' said Pockle.

'Any ideas?' asked Brynhild.

Bienia didn't like to admit it, but she knew little to nothing of the lands south of Asterland. Maybe Maena did. 'Hevac? Any clue?'

Hevac rubbed his beard, then stopped. He almost looked surprised to find it there.

'That's a no then,' said Brynhild.

'They are likely from the lands to the south,' said Hevac.

Brynhild chuckled. 'Well, duh.'

Hevac gave Brynhild a cold look. 'The Arann empire broke many years ago. It will most likely be a warlord's army off to conquer Asterland.'

'Just brilliant,' said Brynhild.

'It is not our concern. We have a more important task to complete,' said Hevac.

'Yes, yes. We get it. Defeat Oberon, save the world,' said Brynhild.

'My brother is right. We must maintain focus,' said Neave.

If anyone other than Bienia had noticed Neave's slight hesitation before calling Hevac her brother, they did not say anything.

'I'm sure the Astish army will be able to handle it,' said Bienia.

Brynhild shrugged. 'I don't suppose there is a lot we can do about it anyhow.'

'Then we are agreed?' asked Hevac.

'We are. Next stop... Uh, where was it again?' Bienia was slightly embarrassed that she couldn't remember the name of their destination.

'Kadrath. Feybane is in Emperor Yavin's tomb in northern Kadrath, on the southern border of the Pockveld,' said Hevac.

Bienia adjusted the straps on her backpack. 'No sense in hanging around. Let's go.'

CHAPTER 27

The news of the approaching Astish army spread around the warlord's host like wildfire. A group of nomad scouts had returned with news of the force mid-afternoon, and it was soon clear that a battle would be fought the following day. Julienne found John leaving the latrines and pulled him to one side.

'You heard the news?' asked Julienne.

'Me and the rest of the army. Are you going to tell me the plan now?' asked John.

'What advantage does the warlord's army have over King Stephen's?' asked Julienne.

'He has more soldiers.'

'Yes. Specifically, many slave-soldiers.'

'So?'

'Slave-soldiers are not fighting out of a sense of loyalty to King or country,' said Julienne.

'The spear-sergeants make sure they fight.'

'What if I told you I know a spear-sergeant who is willing to switch sides?'

'I would say you are full of shit,' said John.

Julienne smiled. 'Have some faith. Spear-sergeant Valun would do anything for me.'

John felt a twinge of jealousy. He had seen them together, and it didn't feel good to have his suspicions confirmed. 'Anything?'

'Are you jealous, John Cotterill?' Julienne stepped closer and took his hands in hers.

'Might be.'

Julienne kissed his cheek. 'You're my man. Valun is just work.'

John sighed. 'I know. I don't have to like it though.'

'It's sweet that you don't.'

John tried to put the thought of Julienne and Valun together out of his mind. 'What do you need me to do?'

'Bring any soldiers you can to meet with Valun's spear during the battle. He'll be raising an Astish flag as a signal.'

'Where did you get one of those?'

'Fort May. Valun took it as a trophy.'

'Huh.'

'I've sent word about our plan, so King Stephen can take advantage of the confusion when one of the spears switches sides.'

'It sounds dangerous.'

'Yes it is. But Valun is very brave and very devoted. Plus, I may have let slip that there may be a few Lordships going after the rebellion is put down. As well as brave and devoted, he is very ambitious.'

'We'll be ready,' said John.

'I will be with Valun to make sure he doesn't back out.'

'Julienne.' John squeezed her hands. 'Be careful.'

'Always.' She pulled him down into a long kiss. 'See you tomorrow.'

Spear-sergeant Jak shouted them all awake before dawn. There was much stumbling about and cursing as the men found their weapons and assembled. John, Jimmy, Eric and Guzzai made sure they were together. John had shared the details of Julienne's plan the previous night and, despite a few voiced misgivings, they were now determined to go through with it, to fight for Asterland and win their freedom and a big bag of gold.

'Gods, I'm so fecking nervous,' said Jimmy.

'Pre-battle nerves. You'll be okay,' said Eric.

'I am nervous too my friends. This is not normal battle,' said Guzzai.

'Just be ready. When we see the Astish flag raised by Valun, we go and join them.'

'I still can't believe it,' said Eric. 'Your woman must be something else.'

John didn't like the direction this conversation was going. Fortunately, several loud blasts on the host's war-horns cut it short, and drums started to pound a steady rhythm.

He gripped his spear and waited, the thump of the drums shaking his bones. Then the host was moving forward.

After a couple of minutes of a slow and steady advance, a roar went up from the throats of the host's vanguard and the armies crashed together. The sounds of steel on steel and the cries of the wounded and dying filled the air.

John cast a sideways glance at Jimmy. The young sailor was looking pale.

John leaned in and asked, 'You okay?'

Jimmy looked at him. 'Seriously? No.'

'Just try not to shit self, okay? Last thing you want is to be smelling of shit all day,' said Guzzai.

'No, the last thing I want is to bloody be here in the middle of a sodding battle,' said Jimmy.

'Just keep it together and watch out for that flag,' said John.

Jimmy nodded and shifted his grip on his spear.

The noise of battle intensified as they got closer to the battle line until their spear came to a halt, waiting to reinforce the line as required.

'There!' Eric pointed.

John followed Eric's finger and saw an Astish flag hoisted into the sky on the left flank somewhere. He couldn't see much else from where they were.

'Come on, let's go,' said John.

The four of them started moving towards the flag. As long as they didn't try to go backwards, nobody seemed to have a problem with them making their way through the ranks of slave-soldiers.

After what seemed an age, they finally worked their way to the edge of the spear's formation and could see what was happening. The left flank was in chaos. Astish cavalry had charged and instead of being met by a bristling wall of spears, the slave-soldiers had moved aside, lifted their spears and let the cavalry through to the unprepared mercenaries behind them. The slave-soldiers that had made up the front of the warlord's left flank were now following the cavalry and butchering the disorganised men who had been surprised by the cavalry assault. The officers in the centre had only just realised their danger and were hastily trying to get a line of soldiers facing towards what had been the host's left flank.

'We have to get over there. Now,' said John.

He led the way as they left the mass of troops and scuttled across open ground towards the massacre.

As they neared the slave-soldiers now fighting for the Astish, John raised his right fist and shouted, 'We are with you!'

He was surprised when he heard the shout being echoed by many others and glanced left and right to see that they had been followed by at least two dozen slave-soldiers from the central formation.

When they reached the spearmen under the Astish flag, they were greeted with back slaps and smiles. It seemed fighting against the warlord's host was more popular than fighting for it among the slave-soldiers.

After the impact of the Astish cavalry charge, the mercenaries had lost all semblance of cohesion and were now running for their lives while being chased and scythed down by the men on horseback.

'Bloody hell,' said Jimmy.

'Yes, this is bloody great!' There was an almost maniacal tinge to Guzzai's laugh. He pointed back towards the middle of the battlefield. 'Look! The Astish are crushing them.'

It was true. John saw that the Astish infantry had smashed into the centre of the warlord's army and that centre was already buckling on its left side as men started fading away when they became aware of the rampant Astish cavalry and the renegade spear of slave-soldiers on their left. The host's officers were trying to keep things together, but more and more men were ignoring them, throwing down their spears and running.

Spear-sergeant Valun's voice cut across the din of battle. 'Deadly viper formation!'

The spear-soldiers quickly formed up, presenting a prickly wall of spear points aimed at the disorganised chaos that was the warlord's host.

The three of them were a few ranks back surrounded by their fellow sweaty soldiers.

'Glad we're not in the front,' said Jimmy.

Then, Valun shouted, 'Advance!'

The tramp of booted feet striking the ground in unison made John's spine tingle. It made him feel part of something powerful.

'We will gut them!' Guzzai's eyes were wild and excited.

Eric's eyes were more haunted and grim, while Jimmy's were nervous and pensive.

John didn't get much time to wonder what his eyes looked like before the 'deadly viper formation' drove into the disintegrating flank of the warlord's army.

The screams of the injured and dying joined the battle-cries of the spear soldiers as they punctured and sliced their way through their former comrades.

John stumbled, steadying himself on Jimmy's arm. When he looked down, he saw that he had put his boot onto the face of a fallen soldier. The man feebly brought an arm up, trying to bat away John's leg, then was still.

The smell of blood and excrement filled John's nostrils as he was pulled along by Jimmy, away from the fallen man. He stumbled on, in a bit of a daze. This was so different from the last battle he had been in. Then, he had been firing a crossbow at a distant enemy. Here, he was tripping over corpses and could smell death. He couldn't see much, the three of them were in the middle of a press of bodies as the spear-soldiers advanced. He could only assume the battle was going well as they were still moving forward and stepping over more and more of the enemy dead and dying.

Their slow advance then slowed and stopped. John could see a large group of men on horseback milling around in the open space behind the warlord's host.

'Are they ours?' asked Jimmy.

'They look like nomads to me,' said Eric.

John could see that the nomad horsemen were splitting their attention between the slave-soldiers still loyal to warlord Karvarl and the mounted Astish men-at-arms who were regrouping after butchering the mercenary companies that used to be on the left flank.

'Are they going to charge us?' asked Jimmy.

Eric shook his head. 'I doubt it, they'd put themselves on our spears and leave themselves open to a counter charge from our cavalry.'

Several of the nomads were gesticulating wildly as they talked to each other.

'I think they are discussing it now,' said John.

The nomads then seemed to come to a collective decision, turned their mounts south and rode, leaving the battlefield and the rest of warlord Karvarl's force behind.

Cheering ran through Valun's spear like a wave, and they surged forward with renewed vigour.

The sound of combat in front of them was louder and John saw an enemy spear shoved between the two men in front of him.

'Here we go,' said Guzzai.

There was a cry as one of the men in front of them fell to his knees, a spear protruding from his torso.

With a roar, Guzzai leapt forward, thrusting his own spear into the body of the man trying to retrieve the spear from the fallen soldier. Guzzai let go of his spear, drew his sword, put one foot on the stricken man and launched himself at the startled soldier behind him.

Eric stepped forward with his spear, stabbing at the soldier to Guzzai's right. 'Come on!'

After only a moment's hesitation, John followed his lead, using his spear to fend off the soldier to Guzzai's left while he wrestled his opponent to the floor.

Guzzai ripped at his opponents stomach with his blade, spilling his intestines onto the dusty ground. Then he clambered to his feet, spattered in gore and looking for his next foe.

The next foe in question took one look at the blood soaked visage of Guzzai, dropped his spear and turned to flee. With a guttural howl, Guzzai flung himself at the retreating man, wrapped his arms around his legs and brought him to the ground. Straddling his target, having left his sword in his previous victim, Guzzai proceeded to smash his fist into the back of the man's head, driving his face into the dirt. After a second blow, the man stopped struggling and Guzzai dropped forward onto his hands and knees, panting with exertion.

'I'm glad he's on our side,' said Jimmy.

John grunted an acknowledgment as he fended off a blow aimed at Guzzai by the man on his left.

Guzzai, having recovered enough to take notice of this, grabbed a sword from the dusty ground and got to his feet with the weapon clenched in his right fist.

The man desperately tried to lift his spear back into a more defensive position but was too slow. Guzzai stepped in close and slid his sword up through the man's stomach and into his ribcage.

Blood bubbled out of the man's mouth and Guzzai tipped him, lifeless, off the end of his sword. Guzzai frowned as he looked around for another victim and found none within reach.

'They're running,' said Eric.

John saw that this was true. Most of the slave-soldiers opposing them had dropped their spears and were running for their lives, and those that weren't had actually joined the defectors.

'It's over? Thank the gods,' said Jimmy.

'It's not over yet. There's warlord Karvarl's pact warriors to deal with.' Eric pointed to a distant banner. It was red and decorated with a stylised green claw.

As they watched, the banner wavered a moment and then fell out of sight.

'Looks like they're dealt with,' said John.

Eric laughed. 'By the gods, we actually won! I'll be making a sacrifice to the gods later, that's for sure.'

Guzzai, although he was covered in the blood of his foes, seemed to have calmed down. He carefully wiped his sword clean before returning it to its battered sheath. 'We have won a great battle.'

'I'm just glad it's over,' said Jimmy.

John agreed. If this was a great battle, you could keep it. It was then that he remembered Julienne must be amongst this lot somewhere. She said she would be with spear-sergeant Valun, so should be safe, but that didn't stop him from worrying.

'I have to find Julienne.'

'Who?' asked Eric.

'Adele. He means Adele,' said Jimmy.

'Yes. Adele,' said John.

He didn't suppose the slip mattered now.

Julienne was pleased that the betrayal had swung the battle in Asterland's favour. It vindicated all the effort she had put in getting Valun onside. The man, although a little vain, was decent enough and didn't mistreat his spear-soldiers too much. She stood silently beside Valun as he attempted a head count of his spear.

'Huh. There seems to be more than before the battle,' said Valun.

Julienne hoped that John was one of the extras.

'You are so inspiring that men from other spears have followed you.' Julienne delivered a perfectly judged dose of ego stroking.

Valun put his arm around Julienne. 'And your King will reward me?'

'Of course, my love. How could he not?'

Valun smiled a self-satisfied smile. 'Then now we go and claim my reward.'

'And the men can go free,' said Julienne.

'Yes, yes. They can go free. After I have the Astish King's favour.'

Julienne hugged his arm. 'Of course.' She sighed happily. Everything seemed to be coming together nicely. The warlord's army was defeated and John would be freed. Perhaps now they could get back to enjoying some time together in Aston. She idly wondered how much hazard pay they had accumulated on this mission, and if it would be enough for at least a month of high living.

CHAPTER 28

Mighty marble columns lined the path leading to the mausoleum of the emperors. Bienia had not seen stonework this old outside of the halls of the dwarven high kings. The path, slashed by the thick shadows of the columns, was cracked and weathered, tough green plants crowding through gaping holes in the flagstones.

The mausoleum was in the dry steppe of northern Kadrath, some distance from the nearby city of Deran. Deran's ancient crumbling buildings were a decaying echo of the glory days of the Arann empire, and the mausoleum was in a similar, if less populated, state. They followed the path until they reached the double doors which led into the mausoleum. They were made of rusty bound iron, the embossed sigils of the old empire flaked and crumbling.

'So this is it?' asked Brynhild.

'This is it.' Hevac visibly shuddered.

'Is Hevac all right?' Bienia was looking at Neave when she asked this, but her question was really directed at Maena who was still controlling Hevac's body.

Neave looked at Hevac questioningly.

'He is fine,' said Hevac.

'Feels a bit fecking spooky to me,' said Pockle.

'What do you mean?' asked Brynhild.

'Can't you bloody feel that?'

'What?'

'Like all your fecking hair is trying to stand up at once.'

'It is because the vermin is of the fey-folk,' said Hevac.

'I hope you're not thinking of sodding going in there,' said Pockle.

'We haven't walked all the way from the Spiky mountains just to look at it then go home,' said Bienia.

'Bollocks,' said Pockle.

'Just stick with me,' said Brynhild.

'Neave, light the lantern. We will need light,' said Hevac.

Neave removed her pack, knelt and rummaged about in it for a moment before extracting a lantern. While she was getting a spark from her flint and steel, Bienia stepped up, placed one hand on each door and pushed. There was a tortured groan from the hinges as the doors slowly swung open. A soft gust of ancient air wafted past her out of the dimly lit interior. What light there was, was coming from small high windows. The columns which stretched up to the high vaulted ceiling were fixed with rusty sconces, their torches long burnt down or missing.

Hevac moved past Bienia and beckoned Neave to follow with her lantern. As the aspirant moved inside, the flickering light cast deep shadows from the columns.

Brynhild checked her sword belt.. 'Shall we?'

The two shieldmaiden followed the others inside accompanied by a pensive looking Pockle, who flitted nervously around Brynhild.

'So, where do they keep their magical daggers in here?' asked Bienia.

'Feybane will be with the Emperor Yavin,' said Hevac.

Brynhild frowned. 'With him?'

'His remains. He was buried with the blade,' said Hevac.

So this was it: they were robbing the dead. Bienia sighed. 'Light another lantern Bryn, we need a bit more light in here.' Not strictly true, but the shadows were making her nervous.

Brynhild obliged, and the group moved deeper into the mausoleum. They soon came to a row of sarcophagi, each with angular writing chiselled into a polished smooth lid.

Bienia looked blankly at the engraved symbols on the first sarcophagus. 'Well, I can't read this.'

Hevac peered at the writing. 'It says, "The divine Gordu: Emperor of Aravic, defender of the faiths, keeper of the holy blessings, warden of the seven halls" – it goes on like that for some time.'

'I'm glad they had the forethought to label them for us,' said Bienia.

'Not Yavin. We shall keep looking,' said Hevac.

Several ex-rulers of Arann with a similar penchant for ostentatious titles later, they found the sarcophagus with Emperor Yavin's name on it.

Bienia pushed at the lid. It didn't move. 'Bryn, give me a hand.'

Brynhild put her lantern on the floor and the shieldmaidens grabbed one end of the lid each and heaved at it. The sound of stone scraping against stone echoed around the vaulted ceiling of the mausoleum and dust spilled down the side of the sarcophagus as the lid inched open.

The dark recesses of the sarcophagus were lit by a faint red glow that wasn't coming from their lanterns.

'Would someone mind telling me what is fecking lighting

up the inside.' Pockle was peering over the top of Brynhild's head while crouching on her backpack.

Bienia peered inside the open sarcophagus. 'I think that's Feybane.'

Hevac took a couple of steps back. 'Can you take it?'

'Uh, he's holding it.'

'What?'

'The dead emperor. He's holding the dagger. With both hands.'

'Please, just take the dagger, Bienia,' said Hevac.

Bienia looked more carefully at the desiccated husk that was the deceased emperor. He certainly looked dead, but she had heard stories about old tombs and old corpses not being quite as dead as they are supposed to be exacting revenge on would be tomb robbers. What was left of the emperor was dressed in what had probably once been fine clothing but was now black and rotten. The gold embroidery worked into his shirt still glistened with a faint red tinge from the soft red light emanating from the dagger clutched in his hands.

'Right... Here goes.' She reached out and started to peel the emperor's fingers from the dagger's hilt.

There was a crunching noise as one of the fingers snapped off. She gingerly held it up between her thumb and forefinger. 'Ugh.'

'He's falling apart then,' said Brynhild.

'Thank feck for that,' said Pockle.

'Bienia,' said Neave, trying to attract her attention.

'Not now. I've almost got it.'

'Bienia. You should probably be paying attention now.' Hevac's voice this time.

She stopped breaking off imperial fingers and turned to see

what the fuss was about. Coming through the doorway at the far end of the mausoleum, silhouetted against the light from the open door, were several men.

'Bollocks,' said Pockle.

'What do you think they want?' asked Neave.

'Nothing good. They're armed,' said Brynhild.

Sure enough, as Bienia's eyes got used to staring at the light from outside, she could see they carried drawn swords.

The men called out to them in a language she didn't understand. She quietly unslung her shield from her back.

'What did they say?' asked Brynhild.

'They say we're trespassing on holy ground,' said Hevac.

There was another burst of incomprehensible gibberish.

Hevac tilted his head and listened before translating. 'And we must pay with our lives.'

'Of course we must.' Bienia slid her arm into the straps on her shield and drew her sword.

Brynhild carefully placed her lantern on the edge of the sarcophagus, readied her sword and shield, and stood at Bienia's right shoulder.

Hevac stepped up to Bienia's left shoulder, sword in hand.

'You sure, Hevac?' asked Brynhild with a frown.

'I am confident of acquitting myself well in battle, if that's what you mean.'

Brynhild shrugged. 'Suit yourself. Neave, stay back with Pockle. Pockle, keep an eye on her.'

Neave looked horrified. 'With the vermin?'

'Why do I get to look out for the dozy tart?' asked Pockle.

'Just do as your told,' said Bienia.

Neave looked to Hevac. Pockle looked to Brynhild.

'Do it, Neave,' said Hevac.

Brynhild said nothing, just giving Pockle a look, and the fairy acquiesced, joining Neave behind the sarcophagus.

After another round of incomprehensible shouting, the men advanced on the three dwarves.

Maena felt a thrill run through Hevac's body. She hadn't been in a male vessel for many years and the combination of testosterone and adrenaline was exhilarating. She flexed her grip on the sword, feeling the power of hard goat herder muscle augmented by her fae magic. She smiled ferally. Whoever these idiots were, they wouldn't know what hit them.

She stepped forward and swung her sword at one of the men. Her blade smashed aside his feeble attempt to block the blow and bit deep into his shoulder, crunching through his collarbone. The man screamed, and his blood sprayed up her arm spreading a dark stain across the sleeve of her shirt.

As the man sunk to the floor clutching his wound, she quickly glanced right and saw Bienia parry a blow and then slice across her opponent's torso, opening a bloody wound that ran from one shoulder diagonally down to his hip.

Now, Maena was faced by another, more wary opponent, who was taking the time to keep his guard up and study his opponent while a second man moved around to her left, trying to get around her.

Brynhild, to Bienia's right, was being similarly outflanked, and the three of them moved so they protected each other's backs.

Now they were surrounded, and Maena settled back into a defensive posture, watching carefully for an opening.

The opening, when it came, was precipitated by Neave. Maena watched Neave emerge from behind emperor Yavin's sarcophagus. Maena smiled at the men in front of her. The man on her left looked a little perturbed by the smile just before he cried out and stumbled forwards as Neave hammered the backs of his knees with her staff.

His companion turned to face this new threat giving Maena the perfect opportunity. She took it and slid her blade between his third and fourth rib. With a gasping bubbling cry, the man fell, collapsing across the open sarcophagus.

A burst of swearing, some in Aravic, accompanied Pockle landing on the head of another of the men. The fairy then proceeded to do his level best to gouge both eyes out of the man's sockets, all the while turning the air blue with the horrifically creative things he was going to do to him, his family and any pets he may have.

The one man left, who did not have a fairy on his head, started yelling and lifted his sword as if to swing at Pockle. His companion waved his arms frantically, indicating his head was underneath his winged assailant. Finally, Brynhild stopped watching this sideshow and kicked the fairy-free man in the side of his knee and, as he fell to the floor, bashed him on the back of the head with the pommel of her sword.

'You alright there, Pockle?' asked Brynhild.

'A little fecking help would be nice.' Pockle was holding on to the man's hair with one hand while punching him in the eyes with the other. This was not making his victim any calmer and he had now dropped his sword and was trying to pry the source of his torment from his scalp.

Brynhild stepped up and delivered an armoured knee to the man's testicles. He immediately doubled over and fell whimpering into a foetal position.

Pockle let go of the man's hair and flew over to Brynhild's shoulder. 'We make a bloody great team.'

'Yes, we do,' said Brynhild.

'Good, you left one alive.' Maena strode over and grabbed the man by his hair. He let out a small cry of protest. Maena switched to speaking Aravic. 'Who are you? Why did you attack us?'

The man mumbled something. Maena could not quite make it out. She twisted her fist in his hair. 'Louder.'

His eyes flicked open, and he stared up at her, his piercing blue eyes filled with hate. 'We are the order of the holy empire, and we will end you profane defilers.' He spat a mixture of spittle and blood towards her which landed with a splat on the dusty floor.

Maena jerked the man's head back onto the flagstones, knocking him out.

'Wow. I must admit, I'm seeing a whole different side of you this trip, Hevac,' said Brynhild.

'There will be more of them. I think we had better be taking the dagger and going,' said Maena.

Bienia was momentarily shocked at the expertise in violence demonstrated by Hevac during the fight. But, of course, it was Maena in control, not the gentle goatherder.

'I'll get it.' Bienia stopped when she saw that the glow inside the sarcophagus had intensified and was pulsing slowly, illuminating the body slumped over it with an eerie red light.

'Should that be happening?' asked Bienia.

The red light surged, casting the shadow of the prostate figure of their dead assailant onto the stone ceiling of the mausoleum, then started to flash brightly, searing afterimages into Bienia's retinas.

'Ah,' said Hevac.

'Oh,' said Brynhild.

'Buggerit,' said Pockle.

The light flashed one more time and then faded.

Bienia blinked twice, trying to rid herself of the afterimages floating in her vision. Then, she tentatively approached the sarcophagus.

'Careful, Bee,' said Brynhild.

'Thanks for the advice,' said Bienia.

She put her hand on the dead man, intending to push him off the sarcophagus, but was surprised when he jerked upright.

Bienia dropped her hand from his back and drew her sword. 'Gods. I thought you'd killed him.'

'So did I,' said Hevac.

When the man turned to face them, his eyes were open but vacant, and the gaping wound between his ribs didn't seem to bother him. He started moaning. This sounded more like the moan of a man with a hangover suffering in his bed, not someone who has had one of his lungs punctured.

He did not try to dodge or otherwise defend himself when Bienia hacked her sword across and into his neck. He also failed to fall over or give any indication of noticing the ragged gash in the side of his neck. Adding to Bienia's consternation, he didn't even have the common decency to bleed profusely from his severed carotid artery, choosing instead to exude a slow seep of deep red, almost black, fluid that soaked into his shirt.

'What the...' Bienia looked at her blood smeared sword and then back at the figure which started to shamble towards her.

'Bee, the others,' said Brynhild.

The other corpses were starting to move, lifting themselves up onto their hands and knees and finally upright in a slow, jerky parody of life.

'Shit,' said Pockle.

Hevac swung a punch at the walking corpse between them and the sarcophagus. His fist connected square with its chin and its head snapped back with a meaty squelch, hanging on by the backbone and a flap of skin. However, all this seemed to do was stop its low moaning, replacing it with a bubbling sigh from its ruptured windpipe.

Neave rushed over and shoved the corpse with her staff, away from Hevac. It toppled sideways onto the floor, then slowly got onto its hands and knees.

Hevac kicked it squarely in the stomach flipping it over onto its back and then stamped on its face. His boot crunched through bone and spread a mixture of brain and hair across the floor. This seemed to do the trick, and the mutilated body finally stopped moving.

'Grab the dagger,' said Hevac.

Bienia jumped over the body, reached inside the sarcophagus, and tried to rip the dagger out of the clutches of the dead emperor. Suddenly, it came away, and she held it up triumphantly. 'Got it!'

The emperor's skull lifted from its resting place, and it opened its mouth as if to scream before its lower jaw dropped off and onto its chest.

'Run!' shouted Brynhild. She was following a retreating Pockle and was already halfway to the exit.

As she followed the others and ran past the other sarcophagi, she could hear tapping and scratching noises coming from inside them. This galvanised her and she put on an extra burst of speed and finally burst out into the sunlight gasping for breath. Then, she joined the others pulling the heavy doors closed. Inside, the rest of their dead assailants, now upright, shambled towards them, their moans echoed around the mausoleum, accompanied by increasingly louder tapping and scratching noises from the sarcophagi. Then, the doors closed with a heavy thump, shutting the horror inside.

They all looked at each other in silence for a moment. The only sound their ragged breathing.

Then, there was a thump of flesh on wood. They all turned to look at the door.

Pockle broke the silence, voicing what they were all thinking. 'Bollocks to this. Let's get the feck out of here.'

CHAPTER 29

The night echoed with the raucous victory celebrations of soldiers. Not only had they survived the battle, but their side had won. Everyone was drinking and singing bawdy songs, and the camp prostitutes were doing a particularly brisk trade.

John stared into the flickering flames of their campfire. Jimmy, Eric, and Guzzai were sharing a bottle of wine and swapping stories that were getting more and more unbelievable as the evening wore on. John had only been half-listening, lost in his own thoughts.

He felt a hand on his shoulder and Julienne sat down next to him.

'Hello, lover.' She kissed him on the cheek. 'That beard needs a trim.'

John stroked his beard. It was true, it was getting quite heroic, almost rivalling Captain Pollow's. He felt a stab of sorrow as he remembered that the captain was dead. 'I suppose it was worth it.'

'What was worth what?' asked Julienne.

He threw a log on the fire which crackled and popped as it settled around the new fuel. 'All the death, and saving Asterland.'

'Ah.'

'What do you mean, "Ah"?'

'Asterland may not be saved.'

'What?' John looked up from the fire at Julienne's face. He saw a deep frown furrowing her brow. 'What's the matter?'

'I've just been talking to Luke.'

'And?' prompted John.

'Riders arrived with news. While we've been saving the kingdom in the south, the north has been invaded.'

'What? I thought we were at peace with the dwarves now.'

Julienne leaned back from the fire. 'Not the dwarves. Fae.'

'Fae? You mean Coventina?' asked John.

Julienne shook her head. 'They're led by some sort of king.'

'King Oberon? Pockle talked about him.'

'That is our current assumption,' said Julienne.

John became aware that the conversation across the campfire had stopped and all eyes were on Julienne.

Julienne looked back at them. 'The army is marching north. Tomorrow.'

'North. Home,' said Eric.

'Good! I fight for more reward,' said Guzzai.

'Bollocks to that. I'm heading for the nearest port, sign on with a merchant ship,' said Jimmy.

'That may prove a little difficult,' said Julienne.

'Why?' asked Jimmy.

'You're in the camp of the army of King Stephen. Whether you like it or not, you are considered part of that army. You can't just leave,' said Julienne.

'Shit, shit, shit,' said Jimmy.

'If it's any consolation, if you survive you will be paid,' said Julienne.

'If I survive.'

Guzzai slapped Jimmy on the back. 'The gods will smile on us. We will be paid and free.'

Jimmy groaned and held his head in his hands.

'I'll be joining the regular infantry tomorrow,' said Eric.

Eric was a professional soldier, of course he would be joining the rest of the men that formed the core of King Stephen's army. Jimmy and Guzzai would be staying with Valun's command. John wondered what lay in store for him.

'And we'll be leaving you as well. We have a mission,' said Julienne.

'A mission?'

'That's all I can say now. Sorry.' Julienne smiled at him regretfully.

'Just you and me now.' Guzzai passed Jimmy the wine bottle.

Jimmy took the bottle, drank deeply for several seconds, wiped his mouth, and then belched. 'Best get drunk then.'

'You two go ahead.' Julienne stood up and rested her hands gently on John's shoulders. 'We are having an early night.'

John and Julienne had an equally early morning. While most of the army were still sleeping off a hangover, they went to meet with the King's spymaster, Luke. The day's heat was still just a promise in the clear blue sky. To the south, carrion birds were circling over yesterday's battlefield.

Luke was holding the reins of two horses. 'You are clear on your mission?'

'Yes. We get to Aston and assess the situation,' said Julienne.

Luke nodded. 'And you are free to exercise your judgment if presented with any unforeseen opportunities.'

'What sort of opportunities?' asked John.

'If I knew that, they wouldn't be unforeseen.' Luke handed a set of reins to John.

'He understands.' Julienne took the second set of reins from Luke.

'I'm sure he does. You are not the only agents being sent into Aston, but you are the ones with the most relevant experience of the fae. The King is not minded to commit his army to battle with so little knowledge about this new enemy. Bring us that knowledge.'

John put a foot in a stirrup and swung himself into the saddle. 'We will.'

'Then may the gods speed you.' Luke stepped to one side, allowing John and Julienne to turn their horses and start their journey north.

John shifted in the saddle and looked over his shoulder at birds slowly circling the battlefield, selecting their morning meal. 'It's to be more war then.'

'Looks like,' said Julienne.

'Are we saving anyone?'

'What do you mean?'

'By what we do. Are we saving lives or are we just keeping King Stephen in power for a few more years?'

Julienne did not reply. Her horse lifted its tail and let out a steaming trail of dung.

John smiled slightly. It was almost as if her horse was commenting for her. 'Doesn't matter who wins these battles, people still die.' He scratched his beard; it needed a wash. 'The benefit of bounty hunting to society is much more clear cut.'

'You're a King's spy now, and that is not a healthy line of reasoning to follow,' said Julienne.

John looked left and right. 'No-one to listen to us, they're all asleep.'

'Perhaps. Perhaps not.'

John sighed. 'Fine. We'll talk later.'

Julienne looked at him, studying his face for a moment before silently nodding.

CHAPTER 30

Aston had fallen to King Oberon quickly. First, the fairies arrived and filled the night and everyone's shoes with wee. Then, while the city woke to wet feet, the redcaps flooded the streets, spreading chaos wherever they went. With the majority of fighting men in the south, they were almost unopposed, and by that afternoon, King Oberon entered the city, carried in a palanquin made of twisted tree branches, still bushy with green leaves.

Once he arrived at the King's palace on the riverbank, he glamoured all the servants and commanded that a huge feast was organised in his honour.

A week later and the feast was ongoing. Although the city streets were more subdued than when the revelry had begun, they still echoed with drunken shouts and screams as the more unsavoury element took the opportunity to indulge their baser desires.

Barnaby and Sylvie stood on the palace balcony overlooking victory square. It was full of trestle tables laden with food and drink. Minstrels sang bawdy tunes while the people of Aston drank wine that had been liberated from the King's cellar.

Barnaby looked down at his jacket. It was green and covered in gold braid and made him feel important.

'The feast goes well.' Sylvie was dressed in a long, flowing gown of the same green. Sequins had been sewn into it so that she glittered in the moonlight as she moved.

'Yes. Our King will be pleased,' said Barnaby.

'You are correct, Lord Barnaby. Your King is pleased.' King Oberon stepped out onto the balcony between them and put his hands on the railing.

Barnaby was almost overwhelmed by the feeling of devotion he felt whenever he looked at King Oberon. He bowed his head respectfully. 'My King.'

Sylvie dropped into a deep curtsey.

Oberon gently cupped her chin and guided her back to her feet. 'I had almost forgotten how pliable most of you are. Thank you for reminding me.'

John watched the three figures on the balcony overlooking the square. He and Julienne had entered the city that morning, tagging along with a merchant delivering hundreds of wheels of fine cheese from Estershire. The people of Aston had been feasting for over a week, and supplies were pouring into the city. King Oberon had declared a month-long festival, and it was proving a popular move. John and Julienne had miraculously found a small unoccupied table near the edge of the square. The only sign of previous occupants was a tray of small iced pink cakes.

'King Stephen could take the city in a day,' said John.

'Don't be so sure.' Julienne nodded to figures lurking in the shadows. The redcaps were a constant presence, lurking around the edges of places people gathered. 'It's hard to get an accurate count, but they seem to be everywhere. And then there's the fairies.'

As if to punctuate her assertion, a trio of fairies flapped drunkenly into the square, coming to a skidding landing on one of the other tables. After a brief moment of chaos, the people who had been sitting there evacuated, leaving the winged menaces to slurp down tankards of frothing ale.

Julienne swung around in her seat, waving her hands to indicate the revellers in the square. 'Even discounting them, the general populace seem to be onboard with the new regime. How grateful do you think this lot will be with the restoration of our rightful King?'

John looked around at everyone eating, drinking, singing, and generally having a great time. 'I suppose—'

There was a sudden crash as something landed on their table sending most of the cakes tumbling onto the floor. 'Don't fecking eat those.'

John blinked in surprise. 'Pockle?'

The fairy clambered to his feet, scraping gobs of pink icing from his legs. 'Didn't expect to see you here.'

'Mutual,' said Julienne.

'Are Bienia and Brynhild with you?' asked John.

Pockle nodded.

'What are you doing here?' asked Julienne.

'Drinking,' said Pockle.

Julienne gave Pockle a look which told him he'd better start being a bit more forthcoming.

Pockle glanced left and right before fluttering up to land on Julienne's shoulder. She started, surprised by his closeness, then her eyes widened as he whispered something to her.

'What? What is it?' asked John.

Pockle returned to the table-top and aimed a kick at one of the remaining cakes sending it sailing into the air and neatly into a tankard of ale on the next table.

Julienne was looking at the figures on the balcony with a thoughtful look on her face. 'This, my sweet, is what Luke would call an unforeseen opportunity.'

John looked at Pockle. 'What, a drunken fairy?'

Julienne laughed, then leaned in close to John. Her breath tickled his ear as she whispered, 'Apparently, "Bienia has a fecking dagger that can off that bastard Oberon".'

'Oh!'

Julienne sat back and smiled. 'Yes, Oh!'

'I thought she was taking some time off?'

'We were having some drinks with Snorri when bloody Hevac showed up, gabbling about King Oberon.' Pockle glared up at the tall figure of the King on the balcony. 'Still, will be fecking worth it if it works.'

'I thought he was King of the fairies. How do we know you're not working for him?' asked John

'He just uses us. Not as obviously as those feckers on Saltrock, but have you seen what he's done to us?' Pockle gestured at the three cavorting fairies on the other table. 'No fecking self respect.' He belched loudly, apparently oblivious to any irony in his statement.

Julienne fixed Pockle with a steely gaze. 'John does have a point. I think I'd be happier if we could meet with Bienia.'

'I was just getting to that. They're keeping the two idiots hidden from his nibs and fecking sending me to talk to the other fairies.'

John leaned forward. 'And?'

'They all think he's great. Fecking idiots.'

'Wait a minute, who are the two idiots?' asked Julienne.

'Hevac and his stupid sister.'

'They were in Bienia's report. Hevac helped them on Saltrock,' said Julienne.

John hadn't read it. 'Oh, right.'

'Can you take us to them?' asked Julienne.

'Thought you'd never bloody ask. I've had enough of talking to this bunch of wankers anyway.' Pockle nodded towards the three fairies who were currently having a loud argument about whose turn it was to find some more beer.

Julienne stood up. 'Lead on.'

With a final look up at the three figures on the balcony, John followed Pockle and Julienne out of the square and down a side street.

By the time they had navigated the narrow streets and alleyways of the riverside district and reached their destination, John was completely lost.

Pockle landed on the wooden handle of a door and banged loudly with his fist. 'Open the feck up!'

The fairy fell sideways as the handle rattled and turned. 'Arse.' He settled into a hover in front of Bienia who was standing in the now open doorway with her hands on her hips.

'Gods, Pockle. Keep it down.'

Bienia did a double take when she caught sight of John and Julienne.

John waved. 'Hello, Bee.'

Bienia leaned forwards and shot a quick look up and down the street. 'You'd best come in.'

They quickly entered the building and Bienia closed the door behind them and pushed home a large iron bolt. The interior walls were covered in various metal implements hanging from wooden pegs. John was not sure what they were for, but if he had to hazard a guess, he would say woodworking. This was not from any deep insight into tool design, but from the smell of freshly cut wood and the contents of the room: half assembled chairs and other miscellaneous pieces of wooden furniture.

Brynhild and two other dwarves were sitting on some completed chairs at a newly made table.

Brynhild nodded at them. 'John. Boss.'

'Is this Hevac and Neave?' Julienne asked Bienia.

'Yes, it is,' said Hevac. 'We're right here you know.'

'Yes, this is them,' said Bienia.

John noticed a slight hesitation from Bienia before she answered.

Julienne looked Hevac up and down, a smile playing on her lips. 'I see.'

'See what?' asked Hevac.

'Oh, nothing.' Julienne hooked an empty chair over with her foot and sat down. 'I know from Bienia's report that Hevac can be trusted, but I'm afraid his sister is an unknown factor.'

Neave drew herself up in her chair. 'I'm a what?'

'Hevac, would you and your sister step outside for a moment? Close the door behind you.'

Hevac stood, pushing his chair back with a scrape. 'Now, look here you—'

Bienia got to her feet and put a hand on Hevac's shoulder. 'Don't.'

Hevac shrugged Bienia's hand away. 'This woman has no authority over me.'

Brynhild was watching this exchange with a puzzled frown while Neave's was a far more angry one.

'You fecking tell 'em,' said Pockle. It was unclear who he was talking to.

'Everyone just calm down a moment, we're all on the same side,' said John.

'He's right.' Bienia grabbed Hevac's shoulders and turned him to face her. 'We have a common enemy.'

Hevac stared at Bienia for a few seconds before grunting. 'Very well. Come, Neave. We will let them have their little talk about us.'

Neave nodded curtly and followed Hevac out of the door.

The door slammed behind them.

'Is it just me or is Hevac behaving strangely?' asked Brynhild.

Bienia shrugged. 'Hevac? I hadn't noticed.'

Her face was such a picture of innocence that John was immediately suspicious. 'Bienia. What is it?'

Bienia's eyes flicked to the door and then back at them. 'What's what?'

'You're hiding something. I can tell,' said John.

'Are you and Hevac still, you know, playing nug-a-nug?' asked Brynhild.

'I don't see what that has to do with any of you,' said Bienia.

Julienne raised her hand. 'Stop. I'm not really interested in the current state of Bienia's love life unless it affects the mission.' She put her hand down. 'Does it?'

'Err, no?' said Bienia.

Julienne fixed Bienia with her best no-nonsense stare. John had been on the receiving end of that one before and had crumbled every time.

Bienia looked uncomfortable for a moment and then

sighed. 'Look, Boss, I have to tell you something important and you need to promise not to get angry.'

'Angry? Why would I be angry?'

'It's about Hevac.' Bienia shuffled so a chair was between her and Julienne. 'And Maena.'

'The High-Queen? What about her?' Julienne frowned.

'She's not dead.'

'You stabbed her through with an iron sword. I saw that,' said Brynhild.

'Yes, I did,' said Bienia.

Brynhild shook her head in disbelief. 'Shit. You mean she's in Hevac? You have got to be kidding.'

Bienia nodded.

'Well, that's just fecking peachy,' said Pockle.

'Wait a minute. What are you all talking about?' asked Julienne.

Brynhild looked to Bienia. 'You going to tell them?'

'Yes. I think we should sit down.' Bienia dragged a chair backwards and sat in it.

Once everyone was seated, Bienia took a deep breath before starting to talk: 'Maena is controlling Hevac's body.'

Brynhild scowled. 'I mean about before.'

Bienia shook her head. 'That's not important right now, Bryn. It can wait.'

'Let me be the judge of what is important. John, go and keep an eye on Hevac and Neave. Or should I be saying Maena and Neave?'

'Right. Okay.' He stood up. 'I'll just be outside then.'

'Just be careful, and don't say anything about this to them,' said Julienne.

John opened the door and stepped outside, closing it behind him.

Hevac and Neave were nearby talking together in low voices. They stopped when they noticed him.

'Have you been banished too?' asked Hevac.

John kept one hand resting on his sword hilt. 'Relax, enjoy the fresh air.'

'Fresh? Your city stinks,' said Neave.

She was right of course. In this part of Aston the river was noticeable mostly by its smell.

'This whole situation stinks,' continued Neave.

'Neave. Be quiet,' said Hevac.

'But—'

'Aspirant. You will obey.' There was steel in Hevac's voice. It was a voice that was used to being obeyed.

John took a step back, towards the door, his hand tensing on his sword hilt. 'It's true then?'

Hevac rounded on him. 'What is the matter, John?'

'You're the High Queen.'

The tension was palpable. The silence was finally broken by a distant high-pitched scream echoing across the city. It was difficult to tell if it was of pain or delight.

Hevac's nod was almost imperceptible. 'Yes.'

Neave took a step forward, putting herself between John and Hevac. 'Mistress!'

Hevac put a hand on Neave's arm and gently pushed her to one side. 'The time for pretence is over, and we have a common enemy.'

'Perhaps. That will be up to Julienne,' said John.

'Ah, of course.' Hevac's tone was dismissive.

'What do you mean, "of course"?' asked John.

'You are her pet. Obedient and compliant. Bienia sees it. I see it. You, apparently, do not.'

'That's not—'

They were interrupted by the door opening and Brynhild poking her head out. 'She says you can come in now.'

'You should be your own man.' Hevac patted John's shoulder companionably on his way to the now open door.

Neave followed, silently glaring at John as if daring him to do something.

John checked up and down the street to make sure they were not being watched, and then followed them in.

'Close the door,' said Julienne.

John complied and joined the others at the table in the middle of the room.

'Hevac, Bienia has told us who you really are. Maena, isn't it?'

Hevac nodded. 'I am Maena, although part of this vessel remains the goatherd.'

Pockle laughed. 'Which part? The fecking smell?'

'The vermin should keep a civil tongue or I may be forced to remove it,' said Hevac.

'I'd like to see you bloody try.' Pockle hovered in front of the dwarf, just out of reach.

'Pockle, please,' said Brynhild.

Julienne banged the table with her fist. 'Both of you stop. We have a common enemy and if we spend our time fighting with each other, well...' She left the conclusion unsaid.

'Fine. I will tolerate it for now.' Hevac deliberately placed one hand on top of the other, palm down on the table.

Pockle landed on the table next to Brynhild, settling cross legged at the edge of the table. He rested his chin on his hand and glared at Hevac with obvious animosity.

'We are going to work together.' Julienne's eyes moved from face to face, spending a second or two on each. When her eyes locked with John's, the corner of her mouth lifted in an ever so slight half-smile.

Nobody dissented.

'Good. Now, let's work out how we stick this dagger, "Feybane", into this bastard's heart.'

CHAPTER 31

The knife sliced through the pigeon's neck, spilling blood into the wooden bowl on the table in front of Hevac.

'I don't like this,' whispered Brynhild.

Bienia stepped closer to Brynhild and kept her voice down. 'It can't be helped. We need Maena to do this.'

'I still can't believe you didn't tell me she was in Hevac all this time.'

'I only found out in the mystic's library.'

'That was weeks ago.'

'We'll talk about it later. Looks like they are done.' Bienia nodded towards John and Julienne standing across the table from Hevac, a dead pigeon and a bowl of blood on the table between them. Neave was watching nervously from the other side of the room.

Hevac wiped the dagger clean before putting it back in its sheath. 'It is done,' said Hevac.

Bienia looked at Julienne. She was examining her hands as if expecting to find something different about them.

'You are now warded against the enchantment of the fey-cakes,' said Hevac.

'Protection from baked goods. You really do have a spell for everything,' said Julienne.

'The ward will not hold if Oberon takes a direct interest in you himself.'

'I don't intend on introducing myself to him,' said Julienne.

Hevac looked serious. 'Do not underestimate him.'

'As long as you can use Feybane on him,' said Julienne.

'I will not have long when he notices me, and he will notice me,' said Hevac.

'How so? Isn't a goatherd the perfect disguise?' asked John.

'As soon as I start using blood magic, he will know.'

'I understand,' said Julienne. 'How long do you need?'

Hevac nodded. 'Twenty-three seconds will suffice.'

'You will have them when the time comes,' said Julienne.

* * *

John felt something poking at his leg. He tried moving it, but whatever was doing the poking wouldn't give up, so he opened his eyes.

Bienia stopped prodding him with her foot. 'Morning, John.'

'Whassagoddamup?'

'Time for you to go be a palace servant.'

He looked around the workshop. The other dwarves and Pockle were at the table eating some bland looking trail rations.

'Julienne?'

'She went ahead. Said she wanted us to leave you sleeping for a bit.'

'Right. So you woke me?'

Bienia shrugged. 'She's too soft on you. Come and eat.'

John stood, rubbed the sleep from his eyes, and joined the others.

Everyone mumbled their good mornings, apart from

Pockle who swore his. He was sitting cross-legged next to a cloth bag. John could see flickering light emanating from inside the bag.

'I'm fecking looking forward to dropping this on the tosser.'

John leaned over and peered into the bag. He instantly regretted it as a flash of bright light seared his retina. He tried to blink away the after images. 'What the hell is that?'

'Bottle of lightning,' said Bienia.

'Excuse me?'

'The mystics. They gave us a bottle of lightning.'

'How does that even work?' asked John.

Bienia shrugged. 'Magic?'

Hevac nodded knowingly. 'The mystics magic.'

'Doesn't bloody matter. It's going to buy old crotchety pants here', Pockle jerked his thumb towards Hevac, 'time to whip up some blood magic to finish Oberon.'

'Mind your tongue, vermin,' said Neave.

'Oh, give it a fecking rest,' said Pockle.

'Both of you. Stop,' said Bienia.

Neave slumped back in her chair with her arms folded and glared at the fairy. Pockle glared back.

Hevac was smiling. He reminded himself that this was the High Queen, and not just a dwarf that vaguely smelled of goat.

There was a knock at the door. Three taps, a break then two more.

John opened the door to admit Julienne.

'Good, you're awake.' She threw a bundle of clothes at him. 'Put these on.'

John caught the bundle and then looked around at the others awkwardly.

Bienia ushered the other dwarves out of the workshop. 'Come on, let's spare ourselves the sight of John getting changed and go find a tavern to pass the time.'

'Maybe we how could play a few hands of Beggar's Five,' said Hevac.

CHAPTER 32

Entering the palace as servants was easier than John had imagined. Dressed in the homespun peasant clothes Julienne had procured, they simply joined the servants clearing up the ruins of the previous nights feasting. Nobody said anything when they trooped inside the palace with the others to start sweeping and scrubbing their way through the massive building.

By lunchtime, John was exhausted. His back ached and his hands were sore. He had never done so much sweeping in his life.

Trays stacked with fresh baked fey-cakes were brought in to the kitchens for the workers at midday. John joined the others clustered around the cakes and hesitantly picked up a cake. It both looked and smelled good: fresh baked and dusted with sugar. He watched his coworkers eating with obvious relish. Had the blood magic the previous evening protected him from its enchantment?

He saw Julienne enter the kitchens with another woman and make a beeline for the cakes.

Julienne leaned in and whispered to him on her way past. 'Go ahead, eat it.'

He overcame his misgivings and bit into the fey-cake. By the gods, it was good. Light sponge with a hint of some exotic fruit he couldn't quite identify.

'Oh, this is good,' said Julienne through a mouthful of cake.

All around the servants were making appreciative noises. Several of them said how lucky they were to be able to serve the king.

Julienne pulled John to one side. 'The servants all sleep here in the kitchens, apparently. The actual servants quarters are full of redcaps.'

'On the floor again?'

'Everyone seems inordinately happy to do whatever King Oberon asks of them. It's creepy,' said Julienne.

'It is,' agreed John.

'If we snag a place near the door, we should be able to sneak off without anyone noticing,' said Julienne.

'You found out where Oberon is staying then?'

'As we thought, the royal bedchambers.'

'Where else was he going to stay?'

'We had to be sure.' Julienne stretched her arms up behind her, provoking a popping of joints. 'I've got some brass-polishing to look forward to this afternoon, so I'll see you back here later.'

The moon was obscured by clouds allowing the four dwarves to loiter in the shadows near one of the palace side entrances used to deliver food. They were doing their best to look nonchalant despite the two shieldmaidens being fully armoured and carrying their swords and shields. It was barred from the inside. Bienia had tried the handle. but there were no palace guards on patrol. It seemed that King Oberon was relying on the enchantment of his fey-cakes and fear of the redcaps to keep the palace secure.

Above them, Pockle was somehow managing a spot of aerial loitering. While carrying the bag containing the bottled lightning enough flickering light had leaked out of the seams of the bag to make him resemble an oversized firefly, so he had stashed the bottle out of sight on the palace roof.

'I hope they hurry up,' said Brynhild.

'They'll be here,' said Bienia.

As if on cue, the door rattled and opened a crack, revealing John's face peering out at them. 'Quick, off the street.' He opened the door further, allowing them all inside.

Once Pockle had retrieved the bag from the roof, he followed them in and John closed the door.

Julienne was waiting for them, her face eerily lit by a combination of the candle she was carrying and the crackling contents of Pockle's bag.

'Ok, this is it. Follow me to the royal bedchambers,' whispered Julienne.

She led the way through the narrow twisting servants passages, up a flight of steps and out onto a landing.

'Where is everyone?' whispered Bienia.

'Sleeping off the booze,' said Julienne.

'Or getting some rest after cleaning up all day,' said John.

'What about the redcaps?' asked Neave.

'Yeah, what about us?' The voice was gravelly, belligerent.

At the end of the landing, lit by the flickering candlelight of the candelabras on the landing were a pair of squat men wearing blood-red caps.

'Looks like intruders, Burr.'

'Yes it does, Spike. Yes it does.'

Both of the redcaps were wielding a wickedly serrated

black dagger coated in a thick green substance. There was a hiss as a drop fell from Burr's blade and started burning its way through the worn brown carpet.

Bienia and Brynhild answered with the whisper of their swords leaving their scabbards. John readied his broom and Julienne a sharp kitchen knife. Hevac and Neave stepped back, content to let others deal with this threat.

'Careful of the daggers. That acid will burn your skin off,' said Hevac.

'No shit,' said Bienia, warily eyeing the gunk covered blades.

'Deadly as night,' said Burr.

'Deadly as sin,' said Spike.

Bienia and Brynhild brought their shields up and moved in front, forming a shieldwall in miniature across the landing.

'Shields is it? Won't do no good.' Burr grinned ferally, took two short steps forward then launched himself in the air.

Brynhild tried to raise her shield and block, but Burr thumped a foot on to the shield, pushing her to her knees while he sprang higher, soaring through the air towards Julienne with his dagger held in front of him, point first.

John swung his broom reflexively, knocking Burr just enough that Julienne could twist out of the way. The black dagger tore downwards through her shirt, and she shrieked in agony as she fell to the floor clutching her side.

Burr rolled to his feet and crouched, his dagger ready. His eyes flicked from John to Hevac and Neave. 'Choices, choices.'

John lunged at the redcap, trying to land the broom handle on the side of its head but the creature moved too quickly for him, sliding to one side and kicking John savagely in the shin.

John hopped backwards, taking a defensive posture over Julienne as she lay helpless on the floor. 'Bienia, help!'

Bienia had her own problems. Spike had thrown himself at her shield, hitting it with such force that she had been forced back a pace. Now, the redcap was hanging on to her shield, dragging it down while he stabbed around the edge with his dagger.

'Shit.' Bienia hurriedly removed her arm from the shield straps, shoving it and the redcap away. Spike threw the shield to one side and grinned a horrible sharp toothed grin. It reminded Bienia a little of one of Pockle's but larger and more menacing.

'No shield now. Time to die.'

Spike moved almost unbelievably fast, dodging around Bienia's block and striking his dagger against her armoured left leg leaving a dent and a smear of the acid from his blade. The metal started to fizz and acrid smoke accompanied pain lancing through her leg. Bienia grunted as her leg wobbled and gave way and she dropped to one knee. She let go of her sword and frantically started to unbuckle her armour.

'Hurts does it? Don't worry, Spike will end your suffering.'

'Feck you!' Pockle had positioned himself above the redcap and now let loose his secret weapon. The bottled lightning fell onto Burr's head and shattered. The redcap was engulfed in fiercely crackling tendrils of electricity, and his expression changed from one of triumph to pain and surprise.

Bienia finally worked the straps loose and what was left of her left greave fell to the floor with a clatter. Underneath the armour, the cloth of her trousers had disintegrated and her leg had a large red-raw gooey patch which was weeping blood.

Bienia felt queasy at the sight of the wound and looked away. 'Gods.'

Spike was lying on the floor, twitching and spasming uncontrollably. Bienia got to her feet, picked up her sword and limped over to the fallen redcap. She then, slowly and deliberately, placed her sword point onto his chest and leaned on it. The redcap died with a sigh and thick black smoke accompanied the blood which pumped slowly around her sword, dripping and forming a pool on the floor.

Brynhild had finally found her way back onto her feet and together they turned to face Burr. John crouched protectively over Julienne wielding two halves of a broken broom handle.

Burr's eyes widened at the sight of the thick smoke curling from the other redcap's fatal wound. 'What's this? Iron?'

'Iron,' said Bienia in confirmation.

'You're fecked now, fella,' said Pockle.

Hevac and Neave moved in front of John and Julienne. Neave had her staff ready, while her brother held an ornate dagger.

Burr gave a little shrug and lifted his dagger. 'Maybe. Burr will make you pay for his life.'

'Neave,' said Hevac.

Neave held out her arm. Hevac made a small cut in her forearm, muttering words in a sing-song voice as he did so.

Burr's eyes widened and his fingers relaxed, dropping the dagger to the floor with a clatter. There was a bubbling hiss as the acid coating the blade dissolved the carpet and started eating its way through the wooden floorboards.

'Kill it,' said Hevac.

Brynhild frowned. 'But—'

Hevac sighed. 'It is one of Oberon's redcaps. There is no reasoning with it. You will be doing the world a favour.'

'I'll do it.' Bienia limped forward. She could smell its fetid breath as she deliberately pushed her iron sword into its abdomen. Black greasy smoke boiled out of the wound, wreathing her arm in a diffuse sleeve. She let go of the sword and Burr toppled backwards pulling a trail of smoke behind him.

John knelt by Julienne. 'Julienne!'

Her face was white and sweaty, and her eyes were screwed tightly shut. There was a faint smell of cooked flesh and John began to feel sick.

'Julienne?'

She groaned in response. Carefully, he turned her over so he could see her injury. The entire left side of her clothing was gone, the edges in tatters. An angry red welt ran the length of her torso and he could see white bits of rib through the sticky mess of melted flesh. A puddle of blood was pooled beneath her and slowly getting larger.

'Oh, gods.'

'Give me your arm,' said Hevac.

John looked at the dwarf dumbly. 'What?'

'Do it, John,' said Bienia.

He looked at his friend in incomprehension.

'Blood magic. Maena can save her,' said Bienia.

'Right. Yes.' He had forgotten Hevac was actually the High Queen.

Hevac took John's arm gently in his hand then drew the ceremonial dagger across his forearm. A bead of blood welled from the cut, and Hevac wiped the blade in the blood and started to recite ancient words in a low sing-song voice.

John watched as the blood stopped pouring from the wound and Julienne's face relaxed. If you ignored the ruin of her side, she almost looked as if she was sleeping peacefully.

'There. Without a sacrifice I can do no more.' Hevac wiped the blade of his dagger clean on his trousers.

John tore a strip of cloth from his shirt and wrapped it around the cut on his forearm. 'Will she be okay?'

Hevac nodded. 'In time.'

Bienia put a hand on John's shoulder. 'Don't worry about her, John. You go. I'll stay with the boss.'

'Go?'

'You've a job to do. I'll just slow you down.' Bienia pointed at her leg. He saw that the acid had badly burnt her calf.

'The vermin should stay as well,' said Hevac.

'What the feck?'

'King Oberon will know you approach.'

'Feck.'

'If he heard this little lot, he's going to know we're on the way anyway,' said Brynhild.

Julienne's eyes flickered open. Her breathing was laboured and shallow as she struggled to speak. 'Soundproofed.'

John put a hand on her forehead. It felt cool and clammy. 'Soundproofed? Really?'

Julienne managed a weak smile. 'King Peter was noisy in bed. You need to finish the mission.' She grunted and closed her eyes. 'Tired.'

He felt a hand on his shoulder. It was Brynhild. 'John. Come on.'

'Right.' He nodded and stood up.

'Take my sword.' Bienia held out her sword hilt first.

'Thanks.' John took the iron sword and swung it experimentally. It was heavier than a steel one.

Pockle hovered in front of Brynhild. 'Be fecking careful with that bastard, Oberon.'

'I will,' said Brynhild.

'This is all very touching, but we should go,' said Hevac.

Neave stood dutifully beside him, looking at them sternly. 'King Oberon must be dealt with.'

'Then let's deal with him,' said John.

John led them through the palace to the royal bedchamber without further incident. The fact that there were no guards on duty made John a little nervous, although it was consistent with the general level of security in the palace since Oberon had taken up residence.

John paused, his hand on the door-handle. 'You have Feybane?'

'Of course.' Hevac pulled out a cloth-wrapped bundle, and carefully unwrapped it to reveal a small red handled dagger. The blade was softly glowing with a pale red light.

'Then let's do this.'

John opened the door and the four of them charged into the room.

The royal bedchamber was opulent. It was richly appointed with heavy red velvet curtains and fine polished wooden furniture. Dominating the room was a massive four-poster bed, the posts intricately carved with heraldic symbols of the Astish royal family.

John's eye was, however, drawn to what was on the bed. A mess of pink limbs and bodies which was disentangling into three separate people.

'Uh,' he said.

Hevac raised Feybane. 'Aspirant. Kneel.'

Neave knelt in front of Hevac and tilted her head to one side, exposing her neck to her brother.

'Wait, what are you doing?' asked John.

Hevac hesitated and started to lower his arm. 'I—'

A beautiful male voice interrupted them. 'That is a very good question.'

King Oberon stood before them. He was tall, over six foot, with long blonde hair, and was very, very naked. An equally naked man and woman watched the unfolding scene from the bed. They were holding hands.

John couldn't help staring at the fae's heroic manhood.

'Gods, what a monster,' said Brynhild.

Oberon stretched out a hand towards Hevac and the dwarf froze, dagger halfway to Neave's exposed throat.

'Is that you, Maena?'

Hevac let out a low whining noise, his arm trembling.

'So disappointing. So predictable.'

John surged forward, his sword aloft. Before he could bring the sword down on to Oberon's exposed body, the fae held up his other hand and spread his fingers, pointing them directly at him. All of John's muscles seized, and he overbalanced, falling forward onto the floor in a clatter of limbs and sword.

'For clan Ironfist!' Brynhild shouted a battle-cry as she ran at Oberon, her shield raised and sword low.

Oberon switched his attention from John to Brynhild and raised his hand, palm up. Brynhild's legs pumped furiously as she rose upwards in the air and was smashed against the ceiling before being dropped to the floor. John felt his limbs loosen and the feeling start to return to his hands and feet accompanied by a painful burst of pins and needles.

'Lord Barnaby. Deal with them.' King Oberon pointed imperiously at the crumpled figures on the floor.

The slightly overweight naked man got off of the bed and grabbed a brass candlestick from a nearby occasional table. John sat up and desperately looked around for his sword. He saw the hilt sticking out from under the bed. Lord Barnaby was advancing towards him brandishing the candlestick.

John, still weak from whatever magic had been used on him, tried to fend off the incoming blow. His arm was knocked aside as if it wasn't there, and the base of the candlestick connected with his head in an explosion of pain. The last thing he saw was Barnaby turning to face Brynhild before he slumped to the ground, unconscious.

CHAPTER 33

Julienne's breathing was deep and regular. Whatever enchantment Maena had used, it seemed to have stabilised her condition. Bienia gently mopped Julienne's brow.

'That sodding redcap did a number on her,' said Pockle.

'Yes, he did,' said Bienia.

The palace was quiet at this time in the morning, and the silence stretched as Pockle grew more and more agitated, flying back and forth along the landing.

Pockle landed beside Bienia and ran his fingers through his hair. 'Do you think they're alright?'

Bienia said nothing. Her leg hurt like hell and she didn't feel like talking.

'Do you think Bryn's okay?' asked Pockle.

'Pockle, I don't know. I'm worried too okay? Can we just wait quietly.'

'I'm going to check on Bryn. If I stay back, it'll be okay.'

Bienia realised the fairy wasn't swearing. He must be really worried. She was too.

'Both of you. Go.' Julienne's eyes had opened, her blue eyes filled with suppressed pain.

'But your injury—'

'Is serious. I know.' Julienne gasped in pain. 'The mission comes first. Go.'

Bienia lurched to her feet and let out a ragged breath. 'Which way to the royal bedchamber?'

Maena was furious. Immobile, but furious.

'*You will not kill Neave!*'

The stupid goatherd and his familial loyalty. He had made her hesitate and now she was locked in King Oberon's enchantment.

'*You are a monster.*'

Maena strove to bring the knife closer to Neave's exposed throat without success. Oberon's enchantment had locked the aspirant into position, neck bared and head tilted so she was looking up at Maena. If only Hevac would get on board with the necessary sacrifice of the aspirant, the force of two personalities could break the enchantment.

'*I won't.*'

She heard a thump to her left. Although she could not turn her head, she could just about make out the candlestick wielding naked man turning towards Brynhild. The shieldmaiden was struggling to her hands and knees. Barnaby raised the candlestick readying a finishing blow.

It never landed.

A swearing blur of fury attached itself to Barnaby's face, who understandably started screaming incoherently.

'Leave' – Pockle bit his ear – 'Bryn' – Pockle gouged at an eye – 'Alone!' – Pockle headbutted Barnaby's nose which broke with a wet snap.

King Oberon sounded amused. 'What's this? Vermin?'

Maena felt the enchantment briefly weaken as Oberon's

attention was drawn by this new distraction. Her hand moved half an inch before her muscles locked up again.

'*Not Neave!*'

This was getting tiresome, and a little worrying. She could be facing a true death here if Oberon took exception to her assassination attempt. And if he found out she was holding Feybane, her fate was sealed.

Barnaby was now on his knees, desperately trying to prise the fairy off his battered and bloodied face.

'Fairy. Stop.' Oberon's voice carried the weight of command. It was a voice that was used to being obeyed.

'You're not the fecking boss of me!' shouted Pockle as he continued attacking poor Barnaby's ruined face.

Barnaby fell to his side on the floor and curled into a foetal position. Pockle let go of his face and flew over to Brynhild. He landed next to the fallen shieldmaiden and put his hand gently on her cheek. 'Bryn? You okay?'

Brynhild groaned in obvious pain. 'My arm. Broken.'

Maena was gratified to see Oberon surprised. She didn't think it would end well for the fairy, but it was good to see Oberon's will thwarted, if only for a little while.

'You dare,' said Oberon.

'Oh, I fecking dare alright, you overblown sack of shite.' Pockle shot into the air again, ready to do battle.

Oberon laughed.

Pockle rolled up a pair of imaginary sleeves. 'Right. You've asked for a fecking bashing.'

'I think not.' Oberon pointed a finger at Pockle.

The fairy started to scream. It was high pitched and the stuff of nightmares. Then, as suddenly as he had started, Pockle stopped screaming and fell, limp, to the floor.

Oh shit. It's probably us next. Maena strained as hard as she could against the paralysis locking her in place.

'*Not Neave!*'

'Gods, can you not put some trousers on?'

Maena recognised Bienia's voice.

Oberon shook his head. 'Another? Do I have to kill all of you in this ridiculous country?'

Bienia limped into Maena's field of view. The shieldmaiden had her sword and shield ready. 'Try me.'

Oberon just smiled and raised his hand.

'*Bienia, no!*'

Maena knew that Hevac needed to let them do it. She could feel Oberon's control of their muscles wavering.

Oberon gestured and Bienia stopped in her tracks. Maena could see her straining against Oberon's control, but it was to no avail.

Oberon smiled beatifically. 'Lady Sylvie. It appears Lord Barnaby is indisposed. Please finish this one.'

The naked woman, who Maena assumed must be 'Lady Sylvie', pulled a slim stiletto dagger from under a pillow and padded towards Bienia.

Maena tried to move Feybane again, focussing her will on overcoming the enchantment. This is it. If we do nothing now, she dies.

Lady Sylvie put one hand on Bienia's shoulder and drew her arm back to deliver the kill strike.

'*Bienia... I'm sorry, Neave.*' Hevac's voice was anguished.

And Feybane bit into Neave's neck. Maena, her mouth now able to form the arcane words required, started to speak the phrase of undoing.

Oberon's expression was one of disbelief. 'You—'

He got no further as his entire body erupted in a blaze of lurid crimson flames.

Maena continued to intone the rest of the phrase, despite searing pain from a deep red fire rolling up her arm from the hand holding Feybane.

Oberon's scream was loud and long, the sound phasing in and out. His body was also flickering, the bed behind him becoming visible through his translucent body.

Maena was now totally engulfed in the bright red fire, and she gasped out the final syllable of the phrase. Oberon winked out of existence. The only thing to show that he was ever there were the smouldering fire charred floorboards.

The red flames around Maena then flickered out, and with a sigh, she collapsed to the floor.

Bienia suddenly surged forwards as Oberon's control was broken by the searing crimson flames. She winced and almost fell as she put her weight on her injured leg. The naked Lady Sylvie was standing in front of her with her head in her hands, stiletto dagger forgotten on the floor.

'I...' She lowered her hands and stared at Bienia, a haunted look in her eyes. 'Barnaby?'

'Is that him?' Bienia pointed at the naked, curled up Barnaby. He was covering his face and sobbing. He was plastered in streaks of his own blood.

Sylvie let out a little cry and knelt by the stricken man.

Brynhild crawled over to Pockle. 'Pockle?'

He was lying still with his eyes closed. There was no reply. Brynhild gently kissed the little fairy on his forehead, her eyes moistening. 'Oh, Pockle.'

Bienia limped over to Hevac and Neave. Neave was lying in

a widening pool of blood, her throat cut open. If you ignored all the blood and the gory wound, she almost looked as if she was peacefully sleeping.

Next to her was Hevac. Every piece of exposed skin was horribly burnt, and his breath was wheezing in and out, stuttering as if about to fail.

'Gods, Hevac.' She knelt beside him and took his hand.

'Aaagh!'

'Sorry.' Bienia put his hand gently back onto his chest.

'Bienia...I'm...nnngh.'

'Shhh.' Bienia looked into his eyes. Those wonderful deep brown eyes with a hint of violet colouring the outside of the iris.

'Closer. I have something to say,' whispered Hevac.

Bienia leaned in closer. 'What is it, my love?'

Hevac sighed out a string of words in another language, which sounded naggingly familiar to Bienia, and then was still.

CHAPTER 34

John had not known Hevac and Neave long, but they had not deserved to die. Once again, he felt a pang of guilt. He told himself that the feeling was irrational. By the time he had come round, Oberon was gone, and the brother and sister had been slain. A loud pop and crackle from the burning funeral pyres brought his thoughts back to the present. The dwarves had a pyre each, and John could just about make out the body of Hevac on the nearest through the fire and smoke. With a sigh, he turned his attention away from the dancing orange flames to his companions.

Brynhild looked sombre, her hands clasped together in front of her. Pockle was resting on her shoulder. John couldn't help smiling a little at the sight of the fairy. Pockle had surprised everyone by actually being alive and announcing that he would 'be fecking alright'. The fairy seemed amazingly resilient and his burns had healed visibly in the two days since they had defeated King Oberon. In stark contrast to Pockle's incredible rate of healing, Julienne was still laid up in bed. The healers had told John that she would be out of action for some time. Again, he felt relieved that she was alive. Unlike Hevac.

His relief became soured by resurgent guilt, and he looked at Bienia standing next to him. She had been distant and withdrawn since Hevac's death. John hoped that the funeral would give her some closure. He studied her face for a moment; it was unreadable.

He hesitantly touched her arm. 'Bee?'

She looked up at him and he could see her eyes were damp with tears. 'He was brave.'

John remained silent. He didn't know what to say.

Bienia looked back at the pyre. 'He was loyal.'

Seconds ticked by before Bienia let out a shuddering breath then said in a quiet voice, 'He was loved.'

She dropped to one knee and came back up holding a fistful of dirt.

'He was Hevac.' She stepped forward and threw the dirt onto Hevac's pyre.

They stood there for a few minutes more before Bienia wiped her eyes with the back of her hand, sniffed, and said, 'I need a drink.'

Brynhild put her hand on Bienia's shoulder. 'Then we shall have one, cousin.'

'One? I think we need more than fecking one,' said Pockle.

John was relieved to see a slight smile creep onto Bienia's face. It was the first sign of one he had seen since Oberon's defeat.

'Pub?' asked John.

Bienia looked at the funeral pyres for a few seconds then turned to face in the direction of the city, and nodded her agreement. 'Pub.'

CHAPTER 35

Two weeks later, and the city of Aston was returning to a semblance of normality. John and Brynhild had been spending most of their time helping with the hunting down of remaining redcaps. This activity had been turned into something of a national past-time, with hunter teams competing to get the most kills. John had been unsurprised to learn that Bienia was running a book on the leaderboard.

It was becoming easier with the help of the fairies. Pockle had become what passed for a hero among the fairies for his part in ending Oberon's rule, and now each hunter team had a diminutive foul mouthed helper acting as a spotter.

'He's round the back of the sodding outhouse,' said Pockle.

An angry voice came from behind said outhouse. 'Curse you, winged vermin!'

John signalled for Brynhild to go left while he went right. They had tried capturing the redcaps, but the creatures were fanatical and dangerous. A compassionate hunter team had tried using nets to capture a redcap for potential rehabilitation. They had been found dead the next day wrapped up in their own nets and intestines. Since then, the order had been to kill on sight.

'I'll rip your wings off,' the angry voice continued.

John stopped at the corner of the outhouse and adjusted the grip on his iron sword.

He gave the signal. 'Now!'

He cautiously stepped around the corner. The redcap had turned to face John at the sound of his shout and snarled at him, raising his wicked black dagger. The redcap grunted in pain as the tip of a sword poked through his chest and thick black smoke started to boil up, obscuring his face.

Brynhild pushed the lifeless body off her sword with her foot. 'Think that's the last of them?'

'Even if it isn't, I've had enough redcap hunting for one day.'

Brynhild smiled. 'To the tavern!'

Pockle landed on Brynhild's shoulder. 'Now you're fecking talking.'

'You two go ahead, I'll meet you there. I'm going to visit Julienne first.'

* * *

John knocked on the door. A familiar voice, tinged with weariness. 'Come on in.'

Julienne was lying in bed, her torso wrapped in fresh bandages. She smiled at him as he sat down on the stool next to the bed.

'I, uh, brought you an apple.' John held out a rosy red apple.

'Thankyou.'

When she didn't move to take it he put it on the bedside table.

'You've seen Luke?'

'Yes, he came to see me this morning. We're getting extra hazard pay,' said Julienne.

'Bienia will be pleased,' said John.

'He's stashed Feybane somewhere safe.'

'Safe?'

'Wouldn't tell me where. Apparently somewhere we can find it if the kingdom ever needs it again.'

'Do you think it will stay saved this time?'

'What? The kingdom? Probably not.'

John laughed. 'I dare say you're right. Maybe someone else can have a go at saving it next time.'

'What, and we miss all the fun?' Julienne's grin was mischievous.

'You clearly have a weird definition of fun,' said John.

'Speaking of fun. When I'm out of this bed, you can take me to an expensive inn and we can have a nice long—'

'Julienne!' John flushed with embarrassment.

Julienne's laugh was genuine and warm. She punched him playfully on the shoulder. 'Break, I was going to say break.'

'Oh. I see. Of course.' John returned her smile. In the end, things had turned out okay.

* * *

Bienia had just finished playing cards with some locals when Brynhild joined her in the tavern.

Brynhild placed two frothing tankards of ale on the table. 'Time for a beer.'

'I've already had a couple, but thanks, I'll take one,' said Bienia.

'How long is your leg going to take to get better? We could use some help with these redcaps?'

'The doctor said it'll be weeks.' Bienia took a sip of her ale. 'Where's Pockle?'

'A fairy conclave, apparently.'

'What the hell is that when it's at home?'

'From what I gather, they get together, drink, swear at each other, maybe have a fight, and decide between themselves what the policies of the "fairy nation" are.'

'The fairy nation?'

Brynhild shrugged. 'That's what they're calling themselves now.'

Maena's familiar voice sounded in her head. '*Ridiculous.*'

'I think it's a good start,' said Bienia.

'Pockle is going to have a word with them about elections,' said Brynhild.

'*He got that idea from spending too much time with you idiot clan dwarves.*'

'Good for him,' said Bienia.

Brynhild put her tankard down. 'I have to use the privy, back in a bit.'

Bienia watched her cousin weave her way through the bar to the privy.

'*Are we going to tell her? About us?*'

Bienia sighed. 'You know what? I think I might just keep it to myself.'

ABOUT THE AUTHOR

Before realising he'd rather write books instead of code, Richard spent twenty years working as a software engineer. During this time Richard also indulged in socialising through tabletop roleplaying; often as the Gamesmaster and often with a pint of ale! From this was born his passion for, and enjoyment of, storytelling. Richard now spends his days writing and visiting various locations during this pursuit. Officially the local library and, unofficially, the local pub.

Printed in Poland
by Amazon Fulfillment
Poland Sp. z o.o., Wrocław

56024063R00141